HYACINTH

and the

STONE THIEF

Also by Jacob Sager Weinstein

Hyacinth and the Secrets Beneath

HYACINTH and the STONE THIEF

Jacob Sager Weinstein

Random House 🏠 New York

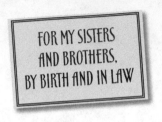

FOR MY SISTERS
AND BROTHERS,
BY BIRTH AND IN LAW

Text copyright © 2018 by Jacob Sager Weinstein
Jacket art copyright © 2018 by Petur Antonsson
Photograph credits: Kiev.Victor/shutterstock (p. 312); AC Manley/shutterstock (p. 314); Alex Segre/Alamy (p. 315); VIEW Pictures Ltd/Alamy (p. 313)

Visit us on the Web! rhcbooks.com

Educators and librarians, for a variety of teaching tools, visit us at
RHTeachersLibrarians.com

Library of Congress Cataloging-in-Publication Data
Names: Sager Weinstein, Jacob, author.
Title: Hyacinth and the stone thief / by Jacob Sager Weinstein.
Description: First edition. | New York : Random House, [2018] | Summary: "When Hyacinth Hayward tries to learn more about the magical rivers under London and how her family is connected to them, she stumbles upon a plot to steal the ancient stones that hold the city together"—Provided by publisher.
Identifiers: LCCN 2017006346 | ISBN 978-0-399-55321-9 (hardcover) | ISBN 978-0-399-55324-0 (ebook)
Subjects: | CYAC: Magic—Fiction. | Secrets—Fiction. | Underground areas—Fiction. | London (England)—Fiction. | England—Fiction.
Classification: LCC PZ7.1.S245 Hyk 2018 | DDC [Fic]—dc23

Printed in the United States of America
10 9 8 7 6 5 4 3 2 1
First Edition

PART ONE

CHAPTER 1

I had saved London, and my mother, and possibly the entire world. I had uncovered a vast magical conspiracy stretching back centuries.

Not bad for one week of summer vacation.

Still, it wasn't enough. I wanted to know *why*. I wanted to know why a group of sewer-dwellers thought I was a valuable magical treasure. I wanted to know why my mother's blood was so powerful that a mysteriously strong elderly lady had tried to drain it. I wanted to know why Mom's memory was supernaturally bad.

Most of all, I wanted to know why my family was linked to the secret magical rivers that ran under the streets of London. I was pretty sure *that* why would answer all my other questions. And if I didn't get them answered—well, I had a feeling that Lady Roslyn wouldn't be the last person who wanted to get her hands on Mom's blood.

When most kids have a question about their family history, they just ask their parents. Believe me, I tried.

I asked Mom, but she had a hard enough time remembering the details of yesterday's breakfast, let alone decades past.

I called my grandma and every one of Mom's eight sisters, and none of them answered the phone. None of them answered my emails. In desperation, I even sent them actual postal letters, which I hadn't done since I was little. I doubted any of them would write back, but Grandma had raised all nine of her daughters to be big on putting things on paper, so there was at least a chance that a handwritten note would prompt some sort of reaction.

I even called Dad in America. It wasn't his side of the family—but at least he was taking my calls. "What do you know about Mom's family?" I asked him.

"Well, Hyacinth, Mom and her sisters grew up in London and then moved to America. And Grandma's parents were from Greece."

"I know that," I said. "But don't you think it's weird that that's all we know?"

"I never met Grandpa Herkanopoulos, but I gather he had some huge fight with his father and cut off all contact. And your grandparents were cousins—which wasn't considered that weird in the old country—so cutting off Grandpa's family meant cutting off Grandma's, too. It all sounded very painful, which is why I always figured Grandma didn't want to talk about it."

And that was it. That was the best answer I could get.

If nobody in my family could explain our mysterious connection to London, maybe *London* could. Maybe if I retraced my steps, I'd be able to spot new clues, now that I didn't have the whole trying-to-save-my-mother-from-doom thing to worry about.

Lady Roslyn and I had entered the sewers through a manhole outside a dusty and faded shopping arcade near Baker Street station, so that's where I started. The manhole cover was still there, as was the battered marble fountain next to it—but the entire arcade had vanished. Where once there had been a large arch, there was now a solid wall.

After splitting off from Lady Roslyn, I had gone to the top of the Monument to the Great Fire of London with my friend Little Ben and a giant pig named Oaroboarus, and it had fallen completely on its side, exposing the hole beneath it where a magical fire hook was kept. The Monument was standing upright back in its usual place, of course, but in the plaza next to it, at the exact spot where the Monument had landed, there was a small one-story building, built out of stone blocks covered with reflective glass. The sign on the door said it was a restroom—but if you were going to build something to stop a giant, heavy monument from lying flat, and to bounce off any magic that hit it, that's what you'd end up with.

Everywhere I looked, damage had been repaired.

Entrances had been sealed. The only evidence of my adventure was the care that somebody had taken to cover it up. And an antique stamp that had still been in the pocket of my sewage-soaked jeans when I finally changed out of them. After it dried, I had tucked it into my cell phone case so that I could look at it whenever I started to think I had imagined everything. During my long day of fruitless investigating, I had looked at it a lot.

So when I trudged up the three flights of steps to Aunt Polly's flat, I was tired and frustrated.

Then I noticed that the door to the flat was open.

I ran inside. "Mom?" I called. There was no answer.

CHAPTER 2

"*M*OM!" I yelled.

"Down here, honey," Mom's voice called from outside the flat.

I followed it out the door and to the flat below us. It had been Lady Roslyn's flat before Inspector Sands and his Saltpetre Men took her away. Now the door swung open, and Mom leaned out.

"Hi, honey! I'm just meeting our new neighbors."

I followed her inside. The flat had the same layout as Aunt Polly's, but instead of being covered with elaborate geometric patterns, the walls were plain white. The smell of fresh paint hung in the air. There were half-unpacked boxes everywhere, with a Manchester return address.

A woman about the same age as my mom stood up from

a sofa and held out her hand. "I'm Zarna," she said. She turned to one of the larger boxes and said, "Dasra, we have another guest."

Dasra popped up from behind the box, his arms full of shirts. He glared at me as though I had done something horribly offensive. "Do you live upstairs also?" he demanded.

I admit it: I sometimes have a problem talking to cute boys, and Dasra certainly qualified. Plus, his posh English accent added thirty cuteness points, easily. If he had been charming or even vaguely friendly, I might have gotten a little tongue-tied. But the fact that he was making small talk in the tones usually reserved for police interrogations made him a lot less attractive. And that made me more at ease.

"I'm absolutely *delighted* to welcome you to the building," I said in the warmest voice I could manage. As I had hoped it would, my friendliness made him visibly more annoyed. Without answering, he turned around and carried his shirts out of the room.

"You'll have to forgive him," Zarna said. "Moving is always hard, and it's been a turbulent summer for us."

I was pretty sure his summer hadn't been more turbulent than mine, but Zarna was being very friendly, and based on the fact that she hadn't yet tried to kill Mom, she was already turning out to be a better neighbor than Lady Roslyn. So I nodded politely and said, "I understand. If you'll excuse us, I wanted to have a word with my—"

"Zarna was telling me that her mother just moved into an assisted-living facility," Mom said.

"That must be tough," I said to Zarna, then turned back to Mom. "If we could go—"

"It's so hard when your parents get old," Mom said. "I'm constantly worried about my mother, although of course she's in perfect health and she never forgets anything. The other day, she was saying—wait, what was she saying? Honey, do you remember?"

By the time I extracted Mom, Zarna had served us a dozen samosas, a plateful of sweet, chewy spirals called jalebis, and three cups of tea (putting the milk in second, I noticed).

Dasra came in and out on various unpacking missions, but he never made any effort to join in the conversation. In fairness, nobody but my mom got many words in edgewise, but at least Zarna and I *tried*.

Eventually, I dragged Mom back upstairs. "You didn't tell Zarna anything about Lady Roslyn, did you?" I asked as we walked in.

"No," Mom said, and for a moment, I began to have a small glimmer of faith in her common sense, until she added, "I completely forgot to mention it. Should we go back and tell her?"

"No!" I said. "We finally have a neighbor we get along with. Let's not make her think we're crazy."

"Whatever you say, dear. How was your day? You were going to do some shopping, weren't you?"

"What? No. I was investigating the whole magical-conspiracy thing. Remember?"

"Of course, dear. I'd have to be awfully scatterbrained to forget that."

I briefly considered about ten million possible responses, but all I said was "I didn't find anything."

"Good for you for trying, though!" Mom said, patting me on the shoulder. "Maybe you can ask your friend the monster if he has any thoughts."

"You mean Inspector Sands?" I asked. "I'd love to, but I don't know how. He didn't exactly leave me his cell phone number."

"You didn't see him at the amphitheater?"

I stared at her. "The what?"

"The ancient Roman amphitheater. Here." She fished around in a pile of newspapers and handed me one.

ROMAN RUINS BURGLED

Stones that have lain undisturbed beneath London for nearly two millennia have been stolen, the *Times* can reveal.

Since being discovered beneath the Guildhall Art Gallery in 1985, the ruins of London's Roman amphitheater have been carefully preserved in their original location. Between 5 PM yesterday, when the museum closed, and 6 AM today, when the cleaning crew arrived, hundreds of stones, forming the bulk of the old Roman walls, disappeared.

"These stones are a priceless part of London's heritage," said Brigadier Valentine Beale, head of the Royal Special Investigatory Corps. "We will not rest until they are returned."

Brigadier? Corps? I wondered. *Aren't those military terms? Why is the military investigating some stolen rocks?*

Accompanying the article was a photo. A square-jawed man in a military uniform—I guessed he was Brigadier Beale—knelt down, apparently looking for clues. Set in the floor at his feet was a glass panel, now shattered. The photographer's flash had turned the remaining shards into little mirrors, and reflected in them was a face that looked like it had been sloppily sculpted out of mud, then decorated with a red line around the forehead. Once, I would have thought it was just a distorted reflection in the broken glass. Now, though, I knew exactly who it was.

"Inspector Sands! Mom, why didn't you show me this before I left this morning?"

"I did show you, sweetie."

"No, you didn't! You showed me an article about a penguin that plays cricket!"

"But that was interesting, too, wasn't it?"

I glanced at the clock. It was a little past four, and the article said the Guildhall was open until five. If I hurried out the door, I could probably make it.

"I'll be back, Mom. I've got to check out that article."

"But, honey, the penguin isn't playing any matches until next week."

"What? No. The one about the Roman stones."

Mom grabbed her hat. "Then I'll come with you."

"Um, that's really kind of you to offer," I said. "But I think you should stay home and make dinner. The key to any good magical investigation is a full stomach. So, really, I'm trusting you with the most important part of the whole equation."

Every once in a while, Mom had a lucid moment, and she had one now. "I know I'm not always as focused as you'd like me to be, sweetie. But you looked without me and you couldn't find anything. Maybe magic is more likely to happen when I'm around."

I wasn't excited about the idea. Mom had a tendency to make a mess out of things, and if I brought her along, I was going to have to spend time looking after her instead of looking for clues.

On the other hand, if I left her at home, she would probably get into trouble anyway. Maybe I was better off keeping her where I could see her. Plus, she was looking at me with big, sad eyes. "All right, Mom. Let's go look for a monster."

CHAPTER 3

$\mathcal{I}$f I were telling you where to find an ancient Roman amphitheater hidden under a building, I'd make a pretty big deal about it. But here's what the sign in the Guildhall Art Gallery said:

↙ Undercroft Galleries

City of London
Heritage Gallery

Study Room

Roman Amphitheater

Personally? I would have ranked the ancient Roman ruins above the coatroom and the toilets.

We followed the signs past paintings and sculptures until we arrived at another staircase. The top was blocked by yellow POLICE LINE—DO NOT CROSS tape. At the bottom, a pair of glass doors led into darkness.

I lifted the police tape and ducked under. Mom hesitated. "Are we allowed to do that? It says 'do not cross.' Doesn't that mean we're breaking the law? What if we set off a chain of events that ends with us locked in jail with a murderer?"

"What if we don't go through and we end up being trapped in *this* room with a murderer?"

"That's a very good point, sweetie," Mom said, and followed me.

We stepped through the glass doors, and for the first time since we left the Crossness sewage pumping station, I knew I was in the presence of magic.

It was a long, dark room, filled with strange glowing people. Rippling lights swam across the floor. The roars of an ancient crowd mingled with an unearthly grinding sound.

Then my eyes adjusted to the darkness. I realized that the glowing people were figures painted on glass. The rippling lights on the floor came from spotlights with rotating covers, and the grinding noise just meant that the covers were overdue for some lubrication. And when the roars of the crowd paused, then started over again, I realized they were an audio loop coming from discreetly recessed speakers in the walls.

It wasn't magic I was witnessing. It was tourism.

A path stretched through the middle of the room, between the remnants of two old stone walls. I don't know how tall they had been originally, but now they were barely three inches high. They had been cut in a perfectly straight line, as if a laser beam had sheared them off.

Farther inside the room, I found the shattered glass panel we had seen in the photograph. I looked around, half expecting to see Inspector Sands, but of course he was long gone. Instead, I knelt to see what the glass had been protecting: a long series of wooden planks. I wasn't an archaeologist, but if my experiences had prepared me to recognize anything, it was this.

"It's a sewer," I told Mom. "The water must have come down this narrow channel, and the muck and sand would drop into this deeper part so they wouldn't clog things up."

"Somebody stole part of an old sewer? There are so many nicer ones. Like the one where Lady Roslyn tried to kill me. That was lovely."

I looked more closely. "The funny thing is, I don't think they *did* steal any part of it. I mean, there's bits and pieces missing, but these edges are jagged, like they fell off over the years. It's not smooth like the spot where the Roman wall was cut off."

Someone stepped outside from behind a pillar. In the dim light, it was impossible to see who it was, but Mom and I jumped to the same conclusion.

"The police!" Mom said. "Don't lock us in jail with a killer!"

"Oooh, is there a killer on the loose?" the new arrival asked. "Are you going to catch him? Can I help?"

He stepped forwards enough for me to see that he was much too short to be a policeman—and in any case, I had recognized his voice immediately. "Little Ben!" I said, and ran over to him.

When we had finished hugging, we both asked at the same time, "What are you doing here?" Then we both said, "I bet I can guess."

"You go first," he said.

"You saw the same newspaper article I did, didn't you?" I asked.

He nodded. "I would have been here sooner, but I only get newspapers when they drift down the drain, and it can take a few hours."

"But why were you hiding?"

"I thought you were the police."

"I'm sorry we crossed your police line! Don't arrest us!" Mom said.

"Mom, Little Ben isn't the police. Don't you remember him?"

"But I wasn't talking to him," Mom said. "I was talking to *them*."

She pointed over our shoulders. Between us and the exit stood a dozen tall men. With their square jaws and their thick muscles bulging under military uniforms, they would have looked like old-fashioned movie stars if it weren't for their complexions, which were a weird, mottled orange. Only one of them had normal skin, and I recognized him from the newspaper article.

"Crossing police lines to trespass on an ancient monument-slash-crime-scene," said Brigadier Valentine Beale. "I hope you have a very good explanation."

CHAPTER 4

A dozen possible approaches dashed through my head. I could lie outright, but when you lied around magic, things tended to explode. Maybe all the magic items had already been stolen from the room, but I didn't want to take the chance. Instead, I decided to go around the glasshouse—to phrase things in a way that might be misleading but wasn't technically a lie. "Oh, is this a real crime scene? That police tape looked like part of an art installation. So sorry! We'd better get out of your way."

Brigadier Beale nodded and waved a hand to his men, who parted for us. As we headed between them, Beale gestured again, and the men closed ranks, trapping us.

"I'm disappointed," Beale said. "I would have expected

more from Hyacinth Hayward. That was not a particularly effective glasshouse."

"If you know who I am, you're not with the regular authorities. You're part of the city's magical protection," I answered. "And that means this wasn't an ordinary theft. We saved the city once before. Let us help you again."

"There's a reason I'm in charge now. Unlike Inspector Sands, I'm no fool. When the same suspicious gang keeps showing up at the scene of the crime, I'm capable of connecting the dots."

"You don't think *we*—"

Beale cut me off by turning crisply to his men. "Arrest them," he barked.

"Run!" I yelled.

Mom, Little Ben, and I all dashed forwards in different directions. I lowered my shoulder, bracing myself for the impact with the massive soldier in front of me. But as soon as I bumped into him, he went flying backwards, spinning head over heels, as if he were light as a balloon.

Okay, that was not what I expected, I thought. Then I thought, *Ow*, because the combination of surprise and forward momentum sent me crashing to the floor. Meanwhile, the soldier had bounced off the wall and careened right back, landing on top of me. He slammed his hands onto the floor, and they stuck there with a wet sucking noise.

I tried to stand up. Given how light he was, I ought to

have easily thrown him off, but his hands were fixed firmly to the floor.

I craned my neck around as best as I could from under the soldier, and I could see that Mom and Little Ben were being held down, too.

"Corkers!" Little Ben exclaimed.

"Darn it!" I agreed.

"No, it's not an interjection. These aren't ordinary soldiers. They're Corkers."

I looked up at the face of the person who had me pinned down. It wasn't a person at all. His orange complexion, mottled with black lines, wasn't the result of bad skin. He was made entirely of cork.

"Let me go," I told the Corker.

Pop! the Corker said back.

What were you expecting from a cork? I asked myself. *Intelligent conversation?*

CHAPTER 5

$\mathcal{A}$s the police van rumbled through the streets of London, I turned to Little Ben. "Can you get a message to Oaroboarus?"

"Definitely! I just need a piece of paper. Oh, and a bottle. Oh, and also a toilet."

"May have to wait on that last one," I said, and went back to trying to slip out of the handcuffs Brigadier Beale had slapped on my wrists before loading us into the van.

I hadn't made any progress by the time the van came to a stop and Brigadier Beale opened the doors from the outside. "Get down," he said.

I thought about making a run for it, but a quick glance outside changed my mind. The van had pulled into a walled yard, filled end to end with Corkers, all standing perfectly straight in shoulder-to-shoulder rows. I could have knocked one of them over, but barreling through the hundreds of them gathered here would have been like trying to make a getaway through a cyclone of basketballs.

Mom, Little Ben, and I climbed out of the van.

"Passage!" called Beale, and in perfect sync, every Corker took a single sideways step, opening up a path to a five-story whitewashed building. I wouldn't have recognized it, because the last time I went through it, I had been unconscious. Fortunately, Art Deco letters over the door told me what it was.

"The Mount Pleasant Mail Sorting Facility," I said as Beale marched us towards it. "This is a good thing. It means we'll get a chance to talk to—"

"Inspector Sands!" Beale yelled, pounding on the door. It swung open, and Inspector Sands shuffled forwards. He was made of mud and looked awkward and lumpy in his Royal Mail uniform, but I was thrilled to see him.

"I ssee you have brought me guesstss," he said to Inspector Beale.

"Some of us don't let suspects slip out of our grasp," Beale said.

"Ssome of uss are more cautiouss in our ssusspiszionss."

"I remind you: you report to me now," Beale said. "You will take these prisoners, and unlike last time, you will not let them get away."

"You have my word," Sands said. "I will sstore them

in a sspesshial area resserved for my mosst dangerouss prissonerss."

Beale squinted suspiciously, as if turning Inspector Sands's words over in his mind, looking for loopholes. Finally, he saluted and marched away.

"Come in, pleasse," Inspector Sands said. We stepped in, and he closed the door behind us, shutting out Beale and his Corkers.

"What's going on?" I asked as we followed him down an institutional-looking, fluorescent-lit corridor.

"Many yearss ago, when there wass more violent conflict among the factionss that ssought to control the ssecret riverss, the government uszed Corkerss to maintain order. They were easzy to produsse in tremendouss numberss, and they moved sswiftly. Too sswiftly, ssome ssaid—it wass common for innocsent bysstanderss to be injured in their fightss. When the Royal Mail wass given authority for en forssing the truece, it replassed the Corkerss with a sslower-moving but ssteadier forss."

"The Saltpetre Men," I said.

"Exszactly. But after the chaoss you and Lady Rosslyn causzed, my ssupervissor determined that we are not up to the tassk. Sshe hass given Brigadier Beale full authority to quassh magical dissturbancsez. And asz if on cue, a disstur-bancsze hass arissen."

"But the wall was stolen yesterday. Why was he still hanging around there?" Little Ben asked. "The thief is getting away!"

"Yess. I suggessted that Brigadier Beale take action by calling in the two young people who had assssissted in the capture of Lady Rosslyn—"

"And the mom," Mom added.

Inspector Sands nodded politely. "Of coursse. The two young people and the mom. Instead, Brigadier Beale chosze to remain at the szene of the crime, in casze the thief returned. Not precissely the dessissive action I might have hoped for. Meanwhile, I wass forbidden to contact anybody. But if they happened to sseek me out . . ."

"You did it on purpose," I said. "You stood where the photo would capture your reflection. But you couldn't possibly have known I'd see it."

"I had faith in your powerss of obszervazion. And there is ssomething about thiss casse that reminded me of yourss."

Little Ben had been quiet, as if he had been thinking something through. Now he spoke up. "It's the blood, isn't it? That's why somebody stole the walls of a Roman amphitheater. Thousands of years ago, they would have been stained with the blood of gladiators."

Inspector Sands nodded. "Anszient sstoness are like sspongess, abssorbing magzic. That isz why sso many of them have been left standing acrosss London. It isz a ssafety precauszion. But it iss only ssafe if the magzic remainss stored. Ssso. Blood. Sewerss. Magzic. I do not know how they all tie together, but ssomeone doess. Ssomeone who hass sstolen ssomething anczient and powerful. Find them, and they may lead you to your answswerss."

"It's a little tricky to solve a mystery with these on," I said, holding up my handcuffed wrists. "I assume your plan was to get Brigadier Beale to bring us to you and then let us go."

"Not quite. It did not occur to me that Brigadier Beale would arresst you. I continually underesstimate human irratzionality."

"But since you're in charge of the jail, you can let us go, right?" Little Ben said.

Inspector Sands took a large key ring from his pocket, unlocked a massive wooden door, and gestured for us to step through it. We walked through into a wide courtyard, surrounded by buildings on all four sides.

I glanced around, looking for the exit, but the only way in or out seemed to be the door we had come through.

"Which way is out?" I asked.

"Alass," Inspector Sands said. For a moment, he looked like he wanted to say more. Then he simply sighed. "Alass," he said again, and shut the door with a boom.

CHAPTER 6

*L*ittle Ben pounded his manacled hands against the door. "No fair! Let us out!"

I didn't bother. I knew from previous experience that once Inspector Sands had made a plan, he was going to stick with it. Instead, I examined our surroundings more closely, with an eye towards how we were going to escape.

The walls around the courtyard were five stories high and featureless. We weren't going to be able to climb over them.

The courtyard was mostly featureless, too, although there were long, dark lines in the dirt floor, as though they had recently been dug up. The lines converged on an old-fashioned water pump, so I walked over to it and gave the handle a few experimental cranks.

As I did, there was a rumbling all around me, and the

dark dirt lines rose up, lifted from below by long wooden pipes. The pipes unfolded as they telescoped outwards, like a giant camera tripod.

When the wooden pipes had finished unfolding, they stretched from the ground right up to the mouth of the pump. I gave the handle a few more cranks, and water gushed out into the pipe.

"Oooh, cool!" Little Ben said. "Is that enchanted river water?"

"Only one way to find out," I said. I bent down and took a deep drink from the mouth of the pump. My lips tingled. "Feels like it." The tingling spread from my lips to the back of my head, and I could feel an inspiration beginning to take shape. But I couldn't quite get a grasp on it.

"You don't have one of your thinking caps handy, do you?" I asked Little Ben.

"No, it was in my carpetbag." Brigadier Beale had confiscated the bag before he put us in the police van.

Mom looked around with an almost satisfied air. "I told you so."

"What do you mean?" I asked.

"I said we'd set off a chain of events that would end up with us locked in a jail."

"You said we'd end up locked up with a murderer, which isn't—" I began, but then I stopped. In a far corner, the dry, solid earth of the courtyard was beginning to bubble like mud in a swamp. The bubbles expanded, shaping into heads of gray-spattered earth, with a red band around the forehead.

Saltpetre Men.

They emerged fully, a half dozen of them in a tight group. Then they stepped aside, revealing a gray-haired woman gasping and coughing. I sympathized. Saltpetre Men could swim through the ground without needing to breathe, and when they brought a human with them, they tended to forget about little things like lungs.

Then I saw who the woman was, and I stopped feeling sympathetic.

"Lady Roslyn!" Mom whispered in horror. She glanced around, looking for a place to hide, and finally dove behind a particularly thick intersection of wooden pipes.

Meanwhile, Lady Roslyn had caught her breath. She looked up and saw me.

"Hyacinth!" she exclaimed.

To my surprise, she looked happy to see me. Was she faking it, so that she could lure me in? She was still surrounded by Saltpetre Men, but I knew how slow-moving they were. If she decided to go for my neck, I doubted they'd get there in time.

"You needn't be nervous," she said. "I see you've discovered the pump, which takes water directly from the river Fleet. We are in the presence of quite a bit of magic. So you may be certain I'm not lying when I say this: I'm delighted to have any visitor, even one who interfered with London's best chance to be properly governed. Other than the occasional visit from my family, I have no one to speak with."

One of the Saltpetre Men pushed her towards me. "Pump," he rumbled.

"Yes, yes," Lady Roslyn muttered. I noticed the bandage on her foot. It was pretty small, given that I had recently dropped a massive piece of industrial machinery on her. *How does she heal so fast?* I wondered as she strode briskly towards us.

Little Ben and I jumped back. But all she did was grab the pump handle and begin pumping it vigorously up and down. As she did, she looked at us appraisingly. "Based on the handcuffs, you're not here on a social call. I'm guessing you fell afoul of Brigadier Beale."

"You know about him?" I asked.

"My grandson keeps me updated when he visits, every Tuesday, Wednesday, and Thursday."

Today was Tuesday, and the Roman wall had been stolen Monday, which meant Lady Roslyn wouldn't yet have had the chance to hear about the theft—unless she was behind it. This seemed like a good opportunity to find out. "What do you know about the wall?"

"I have no idea what you're talking about."

To make sure she wasn't glasshousing, I rephrased the question. "You haven't been involved in anything illegal since you got locked up?"

"The European Union bans hard labor, and I therefore maintain that *everything* about my incarceration is illegal. But as for crimes perpetrated by me, or even aided by me— not a one."

Little Ben and I exchanged glances, and I knew we were both wondering the same thing. She knew far more about London's magical secrets than either of us. If we told her about the theft of the stones, she might be able to give us a clue that would help us hunt them down. On the other hand, I hated to give her information she might use against us.

But back on the first hand, the theft was already public knowledge. She'd hear about it as soon as her grandson arrived.

I gave Little Ben a tentative nod and a half-raised eyebrow, the universal symbol for *I think we should do it. Do you?* He nodded back.

I filled Lady Roslyn in. When I had finished, she looked thoughtful. Finally, she said, "The magic of London is too broad a field for any one person to master in a single lifetime. Alas, the city's stones are not my area of expertise."

"So who *is* an expert?" Little Ben asked.

"I think I shall keep that information to myself," Lady Roslyn said. "If I had broken into the museum and stolen those rocks—which, of course, I did not—my next move would be to eliminate anyone with sufficient knowledge to foil my plan. You are not the most delicate of investigators. While you are within these walls, you are likely to let something slip to a prisoner who might have contacts in the outside world. And when you are released, you and your gigantic pig are certain to go blundering through the streets of London, leading the thief straight to any experts I put you in touch with."

I didn't have much leverage to make her say more, but I did my best with what I had. "You said you don't have anybody to talk to. Well, if you're not going to tell us more, we don't have much of an incentive to continue this conversation."

"Then it's a good thing my grandson is here," she said. She looked past me, and her face lit up with a warmth I had never seen her show before.

In the half second that it took for me to turn around, I had already formed an image of what her grandson would look like.

I was completely wrong.

"Dasra?" I gasped.

My cute-but-surly downstairs neighbor and I both spoke at the same time: "What are you doing here?"

CHAPTER 7

"*Oh*, don't gawk at each other like that," Lady Roslyn said. "Dasra, given what I've told you about this young lady, you can't be surprised she ended up in prison. And, Hyacinth, surely you can't be surprised that an old lady is letting her family use her flat in her absence."

"It just didn't occur to me that—" I said. "I mean, I wouldn't have expected you—"

"To be married to somebody of non-British heritage? I'm an Elitist, Hyacinth, not a racist. My late husband's ancestors held titles in the court of Emperor Subrata at a time when my own forebears wandered Britain clad in animal skins. His claim to nobility was a millennium older than mine, but he never looked down on me. I trust you won't, either."

Lady Roslyn might have been locked up, but she

hadn't lost her ability to fluster me. "Of course, I don't care when your ancestors—I mean, I don't care when *anybody's* ancestors—I mean . . ."

Dasra had been looking more and more impatient, and finally he couldn't hold back. "Come on, Dadi," he said to her. "Why are you wasting your time with these rubbish people?"

"Now, now, Dasra. The essence of nobility is being courteous with our lessers. That said, dear children, visiting hours are limited, and I'm sure you won't begrudge an old woman some quality water-pumping time with her grandson."

"No way," I said. "I want to hear what you have to say to him."

"How unfortunate for you, then, that the right to private conversation during visiting hours is one of the few rights this prison seems to recognize. Guards! I wish to exercise my prerogative under the Maximum Security Enchanted Prisons Act of 1919. Kindly return these two to whatever cells you have reserved for them."

The Saltpetre Men shuffled over to us. Saltpetre Men are slow and awkward, which means they're easy to escape from if you have somewhere to run. They're also incredibly strong, which means that when you're in an enclosed space with a locked door, there's not much point in resisting. "Come on, Mom. Let's go."

Mom popped up from behind the pipes where she had been hiding, and for a brief moment, Lady Roslyn stopped looking like a loving grandmother. Her eyes narrowed, and a flash of cold-blooded calculation passed over her face. Then she caught herself and, with a visible effort, smiled as sincerely as she could. "Cleo!" she exclaimed. "I didn't realize you were here, too. We'll have to catch up."

Mom turned pale and backed away. I couldn't blame her. After all, the last time they had met, Lady Roslyn had tried to drain the blood out of Mom's veins.

"Come," said one of the Saltpetre Men, gripping my elbow as two others took hold of Mom and Little Ben.

"Take a deep breath," I warned them.

"Why should we—" Little Ben began, but before he had finished, the shambling guards had already sunk through the ground, taking us with them.

Compared to the last time the Saltpetre Men had pulled me someplace, this wasn't so bad. I had a nice lungful of air, and the trip lasted only a few seconds.

Admittedly, it was a few seconds of being dragged through the earth by supernatural beings, with rocks and pebbles and roots scraping my skin, and a constant unnerving pressure on my closed eyelids, and dirt pouring into my ears. But when we dropped through the ceiling of the room below and crashed to the floor, the Saltpetre Men's muddy legs splayed out and absorbed most of the impact, and once I had shaken the dirt out of my ears, I was ready to go. Mom and Little Ben must not have heeded my oxygen-related advice, because they needed a minute or two of gasping and coughing.

I used the time to take in the scene. This was an older part of the building than the fluorescent-lit corridors we had entered by. It was even older than the room I had been locked up in the last time I was a prisoner here. The floor was made of ancient wooden planks laid on a layer of dirt that was visible in the wide gaps between them. On either side of us, rusty iron bars blocked off prison cells. The cells all seemed to be empty. Every once in a while, I'd catch a slight flicker of movement out of the corner of my eye, but when I looked at it directly, there wouldn't be anything there.

Where were the other prisoners? Surely, the three of us and Lady Roslyn couldn't be the only ones.

"Come," said the Saltpetre Man again. (Other than Inspector Sands, they were not creatures of many words.)

The Saltpetre Men led us past empty cell after empty cell, finally coming to three that seemed to satisfy them. Each of our guards removed a large key chain from his waist, unlocked a door, and swung it open on screeching hinges.

The one who had spoken to us before pointed into the first one. "You," he said to Mom. "Go."

Mom looked nervously inside. "Don't worry," I told her. "I'll be right next door." To reassure her, I stepped into the middle one without being asked, and I waved to her. "See? We'll be able to see each other through the bars."

Looking reassured, she went into her cell, and Little Ben walked into the one next to me.

"Ooh, cool!" he said, pointing to the rear wall. A wooden pipe ran along it, with a faint mist spraying out of pin-sized holes along its bottom. "I bet that's the water Lady Roslyn was pumping. What do you think it's for?"

I had seen something similar in an interrogation room before. "Magic river water. To make sure prisoners tell the truth."

The guards took off our handcuffs and slammed the doors shut.

The moment they did so, Little Ben and Mom vanished. I could still see into their cells through the bars in mine—but now the cells were empty.

CHAPTER 8

"Mom?" I called. "Little Ben?"

No answer.

There wasn't even anybody in the corridor outside. The three guards had vanished entirely.

I remembered how empty the cells had seemed from the outside. *There must be some magic in the bars,* I thought. This must be what Inspector Sands had meant when he promised to keep us in the highest-security wing. In the part where I had been kept last time, all the prisoners were together in one big room, and let's just say it hadn't ended up being particularly orderly.

Here, though, none of the prisoners could know the others even existed. There was no way they could plot mischief.

As a law-abiding citizen, I was generally in favor of

mischief-free prisons, but now that I was in one, I was start-ing to think a little disorder might be a good thing. But how could I bring it about?

I didn't have a lot to work with. There was a rough mat-tress stuffed with straw on the floor, and against the back wall, underneath the wooden pipe, were a toilet and a rough-hewn wood table with a dented tin cup, a quill pen, a bottle of ink, and a pad of paper.

There were words preprinted on every page of the pad:

I, _____ , hereby swear that I will not escape prison today. Signed, _____ .
[Hanging this signed form on your cell wall entitles you to one day's gruel.]

That explained the magical mist. When you were in the presence of magic, breaking a promise was as dangerous as lying. So by making people promise not to escape in exchange for a meal, they guaranteed that nobody would escape. Or, at least, that nobody would escape on a full stomach.

Well, I wasn't signing anything. I pulled off a piece of paper, dipped the quill in ink, and wrote a message: *Write back if you get this.*

I folded the paper and slipped it into what I knew was Little Ben's cell, even if I couldn't see him. As soon as I let go of it, the paper vanished, just like Little Ben had.

A moment later, a paper slipped through the bars into my cell—from the other side, where Mom was.

I unfolded the message. It said *Write back if you get this.*

For a moment, I thought Mom had had the same idea, but then I realized it was in my own handwriting.

It was the same note I had slipped between the bars.

I picked up the quill pen and shoved it through, but this time, I kept my eyes on the bars across my cell. As soon as I let go of the quill, it popped out on the opposite side, a little higher and faster than it had been when I let it go, and smacked me on top of the head.

Interesting. Maybe the magical teleportation field had gotten a bit out of alignment over the centuries. I filed the fact away in my mind. I didn't see how it could be useful, but every bit of security that didn't work the way it was supposed to was something I might exploit.

I thought back to that flicker of inspiration I had felt when I drank from the pump. *It's worth a try*, I thought, and I went and stood under the wooden pipe. A faint spray of magical river water soaked my hair. Was that the tingling of an idea I felt, or just cold water sinking into my scalp?

Probably cold water. No ideas came, and soon I was shivering. I wished I could brainstorm with Little Ben, but nothing could go from one cell to the next, and there I was, standing under a freezing pipe like an idiot, while—

Wait a minute. The pipe. The water hadn't run out, although small amounts of it were constantly spraying through the pinholes. A constant fresh supply must be coming from somewhere. And the only place it could be coming from was the next cell over.

That must be why the pipes were wood and the bars were cast iron. I knew that metal transmitted magic as well as it did electricity, so the bars must have transmitted whatever magical force hid the prisoners from each other. And maybe wood insulated magic as well as it did electricity, so the wood pipes let the magical water circulate without radiating too much power.

Could I slip a message into the pipe? No—the pinholes were too small to fit anything through, and in any case, the paper would dissolve before Little Ben ever saw it.

There was another possibility: Morse code. I didn't know if Little Ben knew it—but he was always surprising me (and himself) with new skills. With the tin cup, I tapped out a message against the pipe: "C-A-N Y-O-U H-E-A-R M-E"

I waited anxiously. After a few long seconds, a message thumped back: "W-O-W C-O-M-M-A I K-N-O-W M-O-R-S-E C-O-D-E P-E-R-I-O-D S-O C-O-O-L E-X-C-L-A-M-A-T-I-O-N M-A-R-K E-X-C-L-A-M-A-T-I-O-N M-A-R-K E-X-C-L"—

I interrupted by banging on the pipe a few times. "I-F Y-O-U S-P-E-L-L O-U-T P-U-N-C-T-U-A-T-I-O-N W-E W-I-L-L B-E H-E-R-E A-L-L D-A-Y A-N-Y I-D-E-A-S O-N H-O-W T-O E-S-C-A-P-E"

"M-A-X-I-M-U-M S-E-C-U-R-I-T-Y A-R-E-A M-U-S-T H-A-V-E G-U-A-R-D-S O-N A-L-L S-I-D-E-S"

"W-H-A-T A-B-O-U-T B-E-L-O-W"

"O-O-O-H G-R-E-A-T I-D-E-A M-A-I-L R-A-I-L R-U-N-S U-N-D-E-R U-S B-U-T H-O-W T-O G-E-T T-O I-T"

How indeed? I didn't have many resources at my disposal. As old as the prison was, it seemed pretty solid, and I didn't think I could tunnel all the way through it with only a quill pen.

Unless . . . maybe there *was* something I could try. It was a long shot, but it might just get us down to Mail Rail, whatever that was.

"I-S M-A-I-L R-A-I-L A T-R-A-I-N W-H-E-R-E D-O-E-S I-T G-O"

"C-L-O-S-E-S-T S-T-O-P F-R-O-M H-E-R-E I-S K-I-N-G E-D-W-A-R-D S-T-R-E-E-T"

"I-S T-H-A-T L-E-S-S H-E-A-V-I-L-Y G-U-A-R-D E D T-H-A-N H-E-R-E"

There was a pause, and I imagined Little Ben thinking it over. "I-T I-S A-N O-R-D-I-N-A-R-Y O-F-F-I-C-E B U I L D I N G S O P R O B-A-B-L-Y"

That was good news. But just in case there *was* some security there, we'd need backup. "C-A-N Y-O-U U-S-E T-O-I-L-E-T T-O T-E-L-L O-A-R-O B O A R U S T-O M-E-E-T U-S T-H-E-R-E"

"Y-E-S B-U-T M-A-Y T-A-K-E S-E-V-E-R-A-L H-O-U-R-S F-O-R H-I-M T-O G-E-T M-E-S-S-A-G-E"

"T-H-A-T G-I-V-E-S M-E T-I-M-E T-O P-L-A-N B-E R-E-A-D-Y F-O-R E-S-C-A-P-E T-O-M-O-R-R-O-W M-O-R-N-I-N-G"

"H-O-O-R-A-Y"

I sat there in silence for a few minutes, working out the details of my plan. The more I thought about it, the more overwhelming it seemed. I was in a jail built to hold the most dangerous magical criminals Britain had to offer. What made me think I could outwit centuries of protections? What if I was destined to spend the rest of my life trapped in a little cell, unable to see anybody I knew and loved, even if some of them were just a few feet away?

I was beginning to cry when a thumping from the pipe interrupted my thoughts. I listened, puzzled. It was rhythmic and familiar, but it wasn't Morse code.

It must be Mom, I thought. She had heard my tapping and didn't know Morse code but wanted to communicate.

As soon as I figured that out, I realized what the rhythm was. It was an old family lullaby she and all my aunts used to sing to me. The lyrics were nonsense words, but I knew them by heart.

I tapped along, singing to myself:

Ann browsed bridger luna doona,
Eggs feather thorn, a la kenner.

I couldn't see her or touch her, but Mom was right next door. She loved me, and she was thinking of me. And maybe—*maybe*—my plan would work and I'd see her again tomorrow.

I curled up on the mattress and drifted off to sleep.

CHAPTER 9

I was woken by the screech of the iron door opening. A Saltpetre Man stood outside in the corridor, pushing a cart with a steaming bucket of something that smelled like rotten porridge. "Gruel," the Saltpetre Man said, then pointed to the pad of paper. "Ssssign."

Drowsy as I was, I knew it would be a bad idea to promise not to escape. "No, thanks," I said.

As I blinked the sleep out of my eyes, I glanced around. I could see through the bars into the adjoining cells again. Opening the door must have broken whatever magical circuit kept them hidden.

To my left, Mom sat on the floor, eating a bowl of what I presumed was gruel.

"Mom! You shouldn't have signed it!" I called. She didn't respond.

To my right, Little Ben was still asleep. "Little Ben! Can you hear me?"

No response. *My door is open, but their doors are still closed, I realized. I can see them, but they can't see me.*

"Sssssign," the guard repeated.

"I'm not hun—" I began. Then I felt my stomach rumbling and remembered the enchanted mist, and I decided to stick with the truth. "I'm not having gruel today," I said.

He swung the gate shut, and Mom and Little Ben disappeared.

In a moment, he was going to open Little Ben's door. Should I tap out a warning on the wooden pipes? No—since I couldn't see or hear what was going on, I stood a good chance of starting the message before Ben woke up or after it was too late.

Instead, I grabbed a piece of paper, quickly wrote *Don't Sign,* and held it up against the bars. Little Ben would see me as soon as the guard opened his door and broke the magic invisibility circuit.

I stood there holding the paper up until the sound of Morse code on the pipes told me that the guard had left.

"T-H-A-N-K-S F-O-R T-H-E W-A-R-N-I-N-G A-R-E W-E E-S-C-A-P-I-N-G T-O-D-A-Y"

"A-S-A-P B-E R-E-A-D-Y"

"I A-M T-O-T-A-L-L-Y R-E-A-D-Y I H-A-V-E

N-E-V-E-R D-O-N-E A J-A-I-L-B-R-E-A-K T-H-I-S
I-S A-W-E-S-O-M-E"

How to tell Mom to get ready? I once again tapped out a
rhythm, but I did it in double time, so that it sounded more
like a call to action than a lullaby:

Ann browsed bridger luna doona,
Eggs feather thorn, a la kenner.

The rhythm repeated, just as fast. At the very least, Mom
knew I was there.

All right then.

I pulled another piece of paper off the pad, scratched out
the message on the front, and wrote a new one on the back:

I, Hyacinth Hayward, solemnly swear that this
paper is not at the one precise point in the plumbing
system where an explosion would open up a gap that
would let me and my mom and Little Ben get down
to Mail Rail.

At the moment, the note happened to be true. But if there
was a precise pressure point anywhere in the plumbing system, then as soon as the note reached it, the note would be a
lie. Which would make the note explode. Which could open
up a gap that would let us get down to Mail Rail.

I folded the paper into a tight little bar. Then I poured

the remaining ink out of the ink bottle, stuck the paper inside to keep it dry, and closed the lid on the bottle.

"Here goes nothing," I said. I flushed the bottle down the toilet.

Then I waited.

Nothing happened.

Well, it had been a long shot. Maybe there was no such pressure point. Maybe the toilet didn't flush with enchanted river water. Whatever the case, I was out of options, unless I could somehow crack open the wooden pipe and try my luck with that. But without a saw, I had no way of getting inside it.

Unless . . .

I picked up the tin cup, took careful aim, and threw it hard through the bars on one side of the cell. It came flying out of the bars on the other side and made it nearly all the way across, but fell a little bit short.

I picked it up, cocked my arm, and threw it even harder—so hard that I nearly wrenched my shoulder. The cup zipped through the bars, shot out of the other side, and this time made it all the way across, passing right through the bars again.

It came through again, going even faster than before, and shot across the room and through the bars. When it reappeared, it was going fast enough to whistle faintly as it rocketed across. A few more passes and it was a blur, and then a glowing red blur as the friction of the air heated it like a satellite on reentry.

All right. Time to intervene.

I lifted up the table, holding it at what I hoped would be the right angle. Then I thrust it into the path of the cup—

—sending the cup smashing into the top of the wooden pipe—

—and knocking off a huge chunk of it.

Which was exactly what I had hoped would happen, except that I hadn't predicted what the cup did next. It shot into the wall, ricocheting back through the bars on one side of the cell—

—and shooting out the bars on the other, even faster.

It came straight at my head. I dove out of the way, and it carried on back into the bars and right out the other side, faster still.

Meanwhile, the damage I had done to the pipe hadn't gone unnoticed, because the air filled with a loud alarm: *AA-OOGAH! AA-OOGAH!*

CHAPTER 10

*D*odging the cometlike tin cup as it whizzed past, I ducked over to the table, dipped the quill in the pool of ink I had spilled on the floor, and quickly scrawled a new note, same as the old one. Or, at least, same words. The handwriting was a lot messier this time around, because *you* try writing a note with a quill pen while a magically ricocheting tin cup tries to take your head off.

Having already used the ink bottle, I didn't have anything waterproof to transport the note in. I ripped a few cloth strips off the ratty blanket and wrapped them around a handful of straw from the mattress, sticking the note inside. It wouldn't stay dry for long, but it was the best I could do.

I shoved it through the hole I had made in the pipe. "Good luck, little note! Go find a weak—" I began, but then had to stop to dive to the floor as the tin cup nearly decapitated me once again.

The water in the pipe swept the bundle away. I held my breath.

Nothing happened.

Darn it.

The door screeched open. "No esscapess!" hissed the Saltpetre guard, brandishing a pair of iron manacles.

And that's when the floor exploded.

The hard-packed dirt blasted upwards, sending rough wooden flooring planks spinning, bending the ancient iron bars at their bases, splintering the wooden pipes completely, and, by the way, throwing me all the way up to the ceiling. I crashed into it and plopped back down, right at the edge of a huge pit that had opened in the middle of the floor.

With the iron bars warped and twisted, the tin cup came shooting out at an even wonkier angle, lodging deep in the Saltpetre Man's forehead. He didn't seem to notice. "No esscapess!" he hissed again.

All the damage had clearly broken the magical circuitry, because I could see Mom and Little Ben, and they could see me. "Hyacinth!" Mom exclaimed. "Are you okay?"

"Don't worry about me!" I yelled over the still-sounding klaxon, which was now joined by the gushing of water burbling out of the broken pipe and the distant sounds of more explosions. "Get over here."

Little Ben dropped to his knees and crawled under the

remains of the bars, but Mom wasn't sure. "I signed a note, sweetie. I promised I wouldn't escape!"

I had to admit: that was a problem.

On the other hand, dozens of Saltpetre Men were shambling down the corridor towards our cells. That was a problem, too.

Maybe I could solve both problems at once.

"Rip the note off your wall and get over here!" I yelled.

Mom looked like she was about to argue. Then she saw my expression. She grabbed the note and crawled into my cell.

As she did so, the note began to fizz and shake, but it didn't explode. "It's not a full escape until we jump in the hole!" Little Ben shouted, and I nodded.

"Give me the note, and don't jump until I count to three," I told them.

Mom handed me the angrily vibrating note. As I crumpled it into a ball, I looked up. The ceiling had been badly damaged by the explosion; it was sagging, and it looked like it wouldn't take much to make it collapse.

Perfect.

"One . . . two . . . THREE!"

As I called the last number and leapt into the air, I threw the wadded-up paper into the air, too, so that it hit the ceiling as Mom fell into the hole.

We dropped into blackness.

The note exploded.

The ceiling collapsed, sending a thousand pounds of dirt and plaster chasing after us.

CHAPTER 11

$\mathcal{W}$e bounced and rolled and slid down the steep sides of the newly blasted hole, the avalanche I had set in motion roaring behind us. It was pitch black at first, but as we tumbled through a twisty bit, a pinprick of light appeared in front of us, and moments later we crashed through into a Tube platform. Or maybe a Tube platform that had shrunk in the dryer: everything was smaller, from the narrow tracks, to the toylike train that sat on them, to the low ceiling from which a massive roar was thundering.

Wait, massive roar? "ROLL!" I yelled, and we spun out of the way as dirt and rocks and timber came crashing down after us. Within seconds, the largest pieces of debris had blocked the hole we had come through, leaving only a thick trickle of dirt tumbling down.

I didn't fool myself that a hole full of dirt would stop the Saltpetre Men, any more than a pool full of water would stop a penguin. But I did hope that the chaos and confusion of the explosion would buy us a few extra minutes.

Little Ben, meanwhile, was gazing in awe at the train. "The Mail Rail," he whispered. "Even in the 1920s, traffic on the roads was slow, so they built this to move the mail more quickly. They shut it down in 2003 because of budget cuts. At least, that's what the newspapers in my dad's files all said. But I wondered: if it was an ordinary transport network, why did my dad have so much information on it? What was it really for? And what went wrong that they've left it sealed for more than a decade?"

"Let's find out," I said.

On the ceiling above us, the dirt was beginning to seethe and bubble, and that meant one thing: the Saltpetre Men were on their way. We squeezed quickly into the narrow train, facing the dusty, rusted control panel.

"Can you operate a train?" I asked Little Ben.

"I have no idea!" he said. He reached out and began flipping switches and pushing buttons. The train rumbled for a moment, as if the engine was starting. There was a series of pops as the engine died. An acrid smell filled the air. "I guess not," Little Ben said.

"My turn," I said. I was never as good with complicated machines as Aunt Polly was, but she had let me help her restore a 1927 Duesenberg race car once. Now that I thought about it, she had seemed awfully insistent that I understand how it worked—and the dashboard of the train looked a lot like the one on the car. There were a few weird bits (What the heck was a bilge counter? And why would a train have a steering wheel?). But for the most part, I knew what I was dealing with. "I bet this is the clutch. And that's the ignition . . ."

"No esscapess," hissed a voice from above as a Saltpetre Man poked his head out of the bubbling ceiling.

"No esscapess," chorused a dozen other guards, emerging at the same time.

I started the engine, and the train puttered off, a dozen guards lurching after us.

CHAPTER 12

*I*n movies, whenever anybody has to make a getaway by rail, they pretty much win the moment the train starts up, and the only thing their pursuer can do is run along the platform for a few seconds and then stop, panting and shaking their fist. So that's sort of what I thought would happen once we took off.

But in the movies, the train is never a miniature one meant to transport letters slightly faster than a horse stuck in traffic. And the pursuers always have lungs. As we chugged along at roughly the same speed as the shambling dirt monsters behind us, I remembered that Saltpetre Men never run out of breath. They could keep going as long as the train could.

The walls of the tunnel started off looking a lot like the ones on the London Underground—concrete and metal, with wires leading up to glowing work lights. But as we rounded a corner, they changed abruptly to smooth plaster, yellowed like the walls of an ancient Roman villa in a book Mom had shown me once.

Little Ben noticed the same thing. "This doesn't feel like something built in the 1920s."

"Maybe they built the Mail Rail to intersect with tunnels that were already under the city. But where does it lead?"

"No esscapess," chanted the Saltpetre Men.

Painted on the wall up ahead of us was a fresco, the bright colors standing out against the yellowed background. A green garland with orange flowers surrounded nine women, a single star shining above them. The women wore dresses of different styles and colors, and the closer we got to them, the more familiar the women and their clothes looked.

Especially the woman in a white dress with long, fancy ruffles.

"Mom," I said, barely able to speak through my shock. "Why is there a painting of you in your wedding dress on the wall?"

"That's a very good question, sweetie," Mom said. "Honestly, I don't remember much about my wedding. Maybe we hired a painter instead of a photographer?"

As we reached the painting, I stopped the train. The Saltpetre Men weren't more than two minutes behind us— but I might as well use those two minutes to figure out how my family fit into the mysteries of London.

"No esscapess," hissed the Saltpetre Men.

"Um . . . ," Little Ben said, pointing at them.

"Yes. Figure out how to deal with them," I told him, then turned to Mom. "I know you and Dad had a photographer, because I've looked at the photo album. And that's your dress. And the other women—those are the same dresses your sisters were wearing. Aren't they?"

Now that we were right next to the painting, I wasn't *quite* as confident that it showed my family. The clothes matched, but the faces and hair colors weren't exactly right. In any case, the figures were a little too abstract and cartoony to match to any specific person with certainty.

And yet . . . there was something about the *essence* of each figure that reminded me of one of my aunts. Aunt Mel's determined expression, Aunt Uta's elegant poise, Aunt Rainey's arched eyebrow—they all looked out at me from faces that were almost but not quite the faces I had grown up looking into.

Mom seemed to connect with them much less ambiguously. "Look at that," she said, sighing. "Polly's hair is so pretty when she grows it out. She hasn't done it that way for years, though."

"But that doesn't look like Polly's nose."

"Yes, Polly hasn't worn her nose like that for ages, either."

Before I could figure out whether that was a significant clue to my family's past or just Mom being Mom, Little Ben interrupted. "I know how to escape the Saltpetre Men." He pointed, and for the first time I realized there was a crack in the wall running around the edge of the painting. Little drops of water dribbled out of it.

"The Mount Pleasant Mail Facility is built on top of the river Fleet, remember?" Little Ben said. "I bet that's it on the other side. But how do we get there?"

"No esscapess," said the Saltpetre Men. I would have liked to stand there and examine the painting, but they had almost caught up with us.

I remembered how I had gotten through a solid-looking object before, when I was with Lady Roslyn. I took my mother's hand. "Sing with me," I said. As soon as I started, she joined in:

Ann browsed bridger luna doona,
Eggs feather thorn, a la kenner.

"No esscapess," chorused the Saltpetre Men. "No esscapess." They were about ten seconds away.

I thought I saw the crack beginning to glow. Was it just my imagination? No, it grew brighter and brighter. It was unmistakable now.

The Saltpetre Men reached the back of the train and climbed on board.

The glow was almost blinding now, and it seemed to be coming from the women in the painting as well. Was the painting changing? Did one of the women wink at me?

A Saltpetre Man reached out a hand to grab my shoulder—

—and the wall swung open.

Water gushed out, engulfing us all.

CHAPTER 13

Little Ben and I grabbed the sides of the train, and Mom was already holding my hand, so we managed to stay inside the carriage as the torrent rushed past. The Saltpetre Men were swept away, still gargling "No esscapess."

We were safe—except that the water was still coming. The tunnel began to fill up.

"Should we swim for it?" Little Ben asked.

I shook my head. "The current is too strong."

"But if we stay here, we'll drown." He was right. Already, the waters were halfway up the walls, flowing into the train and sloshing over our feet.

We couldn't leave the train, and we couldn't stay where we were. The only solution was to move the train. But with the next station nowhere in sight, it seemed likely the water would be over our heads before we ever got there.

What we needed was a boat. And then it hit me.

"Bilge counter!" I yelled.

"Suffering scalawags!" Little Ben yelled back. "Are we using pirate curses? Ooh, are we summoning pirate ghosts?"

"No, that dial on the dashboard—it says 'bilge counter.' I think a bilge engine is something you find on a boat."

When I had started the engines, I had ignored the dials and levers I didn't recognize, but now I scrutinized them. One in particular seemed significant: a big button labeled TRANSPORTATION MODE SHIFT.

I pushed it.

The train car vibrated and rumbled.

The bilge-counter dial spun.

The water that had flooded the train drained out from around our feet.

And from either side of the train, windows rose up, curving to meet above our heads, forming an airtight seal. And just in time, too: the waters had risen up above us, and we were now fully submerged.

The train floated up from the tracks, and it wasn't a train anymore. It was a submarine.

I put my hands on the steering wheel, whose existence finally made sense. The only question was, which way should I go? Ahead of us, illuminated by the still-glowing work lights, the tunnel curved off into the distance. If we took it, we'd be guaranteed to reach the next station, and from there we could make our way back to the surface.

To the left, the open door led into blackness. No guarantees lay in that direction—but maybe, just maybe, there might be answers about my family.

I steered the Mail Rail sub left, into darkness.

CHAPTER 14

$\mathcal{I}$ turned on the sub's headlights. Slender rectangular fish wriggled through the cone of light, gazing at us with square eyes.

I pointed at them. "Their eyes . . . Are those . . ."

"Ooooh, yes!" Little Ben exclaimed. "They are! Those are postage stamps!"

One of the braver fish swam right up to our windshield, giving me a closer look at the markings on his side. They looked like a few lines of ink that had smudged in water. "And that's an address. Those fish used to be letters."

A big red bag—the kind a postman would carry—swam past us, undulating like a jellyfish.

"I'm pretty sure we're in one of the magical rivers right now," I said.

Little Ben nodded. "The Fleet. The most unpredictable of them all. Oooh, I think I figured something out! Can we go down?"

I tilted the steering wheel forwards, and the boat angled down towards the ground. Except we could soon see that it wasn't the ground. Instead of silt, it was a peeling linoleum floor.

"I thought so!" Little Ben said. "This must have been a sorting office at one point. But the Fleet has always been wild and surging. It must have broken out and flooded the— Look out!"

Ahead of us loomed a squat sea monster with a hundred square mouths snapping. Long arms that looked like hundreds of rubber bands melted together grabbed at us. I wrenched the wheel, and we swerved away from it.

It lurched after us.

I swerved in the other direction, and it lurched again, its rubber-band arms waving and its many mouths snapping right behind us.

It was faster than I'd have expected—but it looked heavy. I pulled up on the steering wheel. The monster tried to jump after us but fell down to the floor with a *thud* that we could feel through the water.

"What was *that*?" Mom asked.

"I think it used to be a postal sorting machine," Little Ben said.

A wall came into view ahead of us, crusted with barnacles that had once been rubber stamps. "If this used to be an office," I said, "there ought to be a doorway somewhere on the floor level." I tilted down, and the headlights picked out not just one door but two.

The first was an ordinary door that you might find in any building, except that this one was hanging loose on broken hinges, swinging back and forth in the current. Beyond it, I could see what looked like a staircase leading upwards.

Next to it was a wide iron door, with a dozen locks and a heavy chain stretched across it. Rust had encroached on the sign bolted to it, but its large letters were still legible:

DANGER. ACCESS STRICTLY LIMITED TO PERSONNEL WITH TOP SECRET CLEARANCE AND ADVANCED DEGREES IN LITERATURE.

Little Ben grinned. "I know which door *I* want to go in."

"We can't go in that door," Mom said. "I forgot my keys."

"We don't need keys," I said. "See how rusty the hinges are?"

"Oooh, are we going to smash into it?" Little Ben asked.

"Not us," I said. "I don't know if the sub could withstand the impact. But I think I know someone who can."

I turned the sub around and brought us back down to ground level. The sorting machine leapt out of the gloom, and Mom shrieked.

"Don't worry," I said, yanking back on the wheel. "Now that we've got its attention, I'm going to get out of its reach and—"

Rubber-band arms shot out, and this time they slammed against the glass, gripping it with little suckers.

"Oops," I said. "Its reach is a little longer than I thought."

The sub strained against the sorting machine's weight, stretching out the monster's arms as more and more of them slammed against the glass. "Fine," I said. "We can't go up. There are other directions."

I swung back down and headed straight for the iron door. As we got closer, the monster's arms stretched even farther. By the time we were nearly at the door, they were shaking with the tension, making the sub shake, too.

The sub slowed and then stopped. We had reached a stalemate.

I kept the throttle on full.

We didn't move.

The sorting machine didn't move.

And then it did. It leapt towards us—

—but now that it wasn't gripping the floor, the tension in its arms jerked it towards us like a giant slingshot.

I yanked the throttle, pointing us up, and we moved just enough to pass over the sorting machine as it slammed into the iron door, knocking it off its hinges.

The only thing is, I had forgotten about Newton's third law: *Every action has an equal and opposite reaction.* And so as we were pulling the sorting machine in one direction, it was pulling us in the other. Which meant that while the engine was moving us a little bit upwards, the rubber arms were yanking us a lot backwards.

The sub shot off, throwing us against the front window (Newton's law again!).

The rubber arms snapped, leaving us free to move—but also free to spin in circles.

Finally, the sub came to a stop. Dizzy, I grabbed the nearest thing to steady myself. Fortunately, this happened to be the steering wheel.

I guided us forwards. As we passed over its head, the sorting machine roared and snapped its teeth, but its newly shortened arms couldn't reach us. I dodged it easily and drove the sub through the broken door.

"I don't suppose either of you has an advanced degree in literature, do you?"

"I'm pretty sure I'm too young to have one," Little Ben said.

"If I do, I don't remember it," Mom said.

"I guess we'll have to make do with whatever education we've got."

CHAPTER 15

The moment we passed through the door, the water outside began sloshing furiously back and forth. Combine that with the spinning we had already gone through, and I was glad my stomach was mostly empty. Little Ben looked okay, but Mom had an expression on her face I had never seen before—her eyes shut tight and her face compressed with concentration.

Mom's signing the contract to get gruel had already resulted in one explosion. I hoped *eating* the gruel wasn't going to result in another one.

The Mail Rail's headlights now showed nothing but bubbles bouncing in the turbulence. Unlike us, the letter fish must have known not to enter these dangerous waters.

"Let's see where we are," I said. We broke the surface, and I waited for the water to finish running off the windows.

It didn't. It kept coming.

There was a burst of light and, moments later, a crash of thunder.

"We're in a storm," I said.

"An *underground* storm!" Little Ben said. "That's amazing."

Every once in a while, when there was another flash of lightning, I would get a faint glimpse of carved stone walls. But with the rain pounding down on the window, I couldn't really make out our surroundings, and the Mail Rail didn't seem to have windshield wipers.

Since we weren't seeing much, I took us back below the surface, where at least the waves weren't quite as strong. After a few minutes, we came to a bend. I steered us around it, and as soon as we had turned the corner, the waters calmed. Shafts of colored light broke through from above.

"Let's go see where that light is coming from," Little Ben said.

I took us back up, and all three of us gasped.

We were in a flooded cathedral, stained-glass windows glowing all around us. The windows at our level were angry, chaotic jumbles of color, but as they rose up towards the vaulted ceiling, they arranged themselves, step by step, into orderly patterns.

I knew where we were. "Every one of the secret rivers has

its own sacred place. I was in the sacred place of the Tyburn with Lady Roslyn. This must be the one for the Fleet."

The waters were now perfectly calm, and the storm was nowhere in sight. I lowered the sub's windows for a better view.

Little Ben pointed to the high, vaulted ceiling of the cathedral. "There are statues up there, between the stained glass. Nine of them. Are those the same women?"

I squinted towards them. "I think so. They're so far away, I can't be sure. And wait—now that I think about it, there were statues like that in the sacred place of the Tyburn, too. I don't know if they were the same ones—I was too busy trying not to get smooshed by them to focus on the detail. What do you think, Mom? Do those statues look like you and your sisters? Mom?"

Mom spoke, although it didn't seem to be in response to me. "I've been here before," she whispered. Her face was still screwed up in that strange way, and suddenly I recognized the expression. I had seen it often, on normal, non-Mom people. It was the face of somebody making an effort to remember something.

"We were all here," Mom said. "My mother and all my sisters. We were arguing. I think we were deciding whether to leave London."

"Are you sure, Mom? You would have been so young. Grandma never struck me as the kind of parent who lets her kids vote on something."

"It's so hazy. *Why* can't I remember? Why am I so use-less?" Her expression changed to one of anguish—which was another thing I wasn't used to seeing on her face.

I put my hand on her shoulder. "Mom, it's okay—"

Little Ben cleared his throat. "Um. I'm really sorry to in-terrupt. But . . ." He pointed up again, and this time the ceil-ing had disappeared. Blocking it was an angry black cloud.

Lightning crackled from it, striking the water frighten-ingly close to us. A massive thunderclap assaulted our ears. As though a switch had been flipped, water poured out of the cloud.

I touched the controls, and the window once again rose up, sealing us in just in time, as a heavy wave crashed into the Mail Rail, pushing us below the surface.

"It's probably time to get out of here," I said. "Everyone, hang on to something. No, Mom, not my arm."

I plunged us deeper, rotating as I looked for exits. The door we had come in by had disappeared; where it had been, there was now only glowing stained glass.

But at the far end of the cathedral were three stone arch-ways, all well below the waterline. As we got closer, I could see that each one had a single word carved above it: *Nu, Whan,* and *I.*

"Which one do we choose?" Little Ben asked.

"Let's take the one I recognize," I said.

We cruised through *I* and found ourselves in front of three more arches, each with its own word: *put, met,* and *hear.*

"How about *put?*" Little Ben said. "It sounds more active."

"That's as good a reason as any."

We passed through to three more arches and three more choices: *my, America,* and *a.*

"So the sacred place of the Fleet is basically a giant underwater multiple-choice test?" I asked. "Let's choose *America.* It reminds me of home."

I sailed us through that archway—and somehow, we found ourselves back in the vast cathedral.

"We must have chosen wrong," Little Ben said.

"That's okay," I said. "We can keep doing it until we get it right."

"I'm not sure we have the time." He pointed to a light that had suddenly begun flashing on the control panel: *Oxygen reserves at 20%.*

"No problem," I said as I steered us up towards the surface. But as we rose higher and higher, it became clear that there was, in fact, a problem.

"Where did the surface go?" Mom asked.

The sub scraped against the ceiling.

"The whole cathedral has flooded," I said.

The dashboard began to beep at me, and the light flashed faster. *Oxygen reserves at 15%.*

I looked at the glowing stained-glass windows all around us. Up at this level, they were astonishingly beautiful, the colored patterns as rhythmic as a song.

I picked one and steered straight at it. It looked like I was going to find out if the sub could withstand a collision.

The Mail Rail crashed into the stained-glass window—
—and bounced off. The glass was unbreakable.

Beep! Beep! Beep!

Oxygen reserves at 10%.

I spun the Mail Rail around frantically, looking for another way out.

There was none. We were trapped.

CHAPTER 16

$\mathcal{T}$he headlights came to rest on a huge carved head. This close, it was unmistakably one of the nine women from the painting. And while she wasn't my aunt Callie, there was something about her that called Aunt Callie to mind. It was her expression—as the sub's light played over it, lengthening or shortening shadows, the face seemed to shift between intense emotion and calm reflection. Both were states I had frequently seen Aunt Callie in.

Mom seemed to feel it, too. She stared at the statue, eye to eye, although the statue's eyes were half as tall as Mom's whole body. "Callie . . . ," Mom murmured. "I can almost remember . . . I met a traveler."

"A traveler? There was someone here besides you and your family?"

"No," Mom said, growing more definite as she spoke. "It's what Callie said. It's what convinced us all. *I met a traveller from an antique land . . .*"

". . . *Who said, 'Two vast and trunkless legs of stone stand in the desert.'* It's a poem called 'Ozymandias,' by Percy Bysshe Shelley," I said. "Aunt Callie made me memorize it years ago. She convinced the whole family to move to a new continent with a *poem?*"

"You know Aunt Callie, dear. She can be very persuasive when she wants to be."

"But why would—"

The beeping became a full-on ringing. *Oxygen reserves at 5%.*

"If you know the poem, you can get us out of here," Little Ben said. "Don't you see? The arches. You have to select the right words. And three of those words were the first three words of the poem. But we chose the wrong one and we ended back here."

Oxygen reserves at 4%.

It made sense, in a way. A family song had gotten me into magical places before. Maybe a family poem would get me out.

We dove back down, and through the *I* arch, and then *met* and *a*, and sure enough, instead of being dumped back into the cathedral, we ended up at three more arches: *traveller, singing,* and *hat.*

Oxygen reserves at 3%.

I chose *traveller,* and we were on our way, weaving from

archway to archway. I recited the poem as we went—partly to help me remember it, and partly because, in my experience with magic, saying the right words out loud could reshape reality. ". . . *Two vast and trunkless legs of stone stand in the desert.*"

As we went on, the arches looked more and more ancient and weathered. Were we just moving into an older part of the cathedral, or was the poem acting like a magic spell?

As we passed through the final arches, I spoke the last lines of the poem: "*Round the decay of that colossal wreck, boundless and bare, the lone and level sands stretch far away.*" As I did, the very last arch crumbled, and we found ourselves cruising along a sandy bottom.

OXYGEN RESERVES EMPTY.

"You don't need to tell me that. I'm already having trouble breathing," I told the dashboard, and then immediately regretted wasting the air. Each breath was a tremendous effort. My vision was fading, too. I felt like I was in a narrow tunnel, with only a tiny dot of light ahead.

Wait—that wasn't my vision. The murky waters around us were actually coalescing into tunnel walls as we pressed forwards. The sand shaped itself into two rails. The tiny dot got bigger and bigger.

Now no matter how hard I breathed, nothing useful was coming into my lungs. I wasn't sure how much longer I could stay conscious. I could see Mom and Little Ben struggling to keep their eyes open, and I wanted to say something encouraging, but I didn't have enough air for words.

The dot was now a circle. We glided through it into a station, and immediately all the water drained away.

With my last bit of strength, I slammed my fist into the Transportation Mode Shift button.

CHAPTER 17

*T*he glass slid down, and fresh air flooded in. Well, relatively fresh—we were in an underground station, after all—but it felt as sweet as a breeze in the park on a summer's day.

And nearly as welcome as the air was the giant pig waiting for us on the platform.

"Oaroboarus!" I said as soon as my lungs were capable of producing an enthusiastic exclamation.

He bowed his head courteously. He was dressed as I had seen him last, with nothing but a bathing suit and a box tied around his neck. As he always did when he had something to say, he stuck his snout into the box, fished around for the right cards, and pulled out a handful of them. Or, I guess I should say, a mouthful of them. He placed them gently in my hands, giving my fingers a friendly snuffle of greeting as he did so.

IT IS A GREAT PLEASURE

TO ONCE AGAIN BE EMBARKED UPON AN

ADVENTURE

WITH YOU

In the past, there had been a few moments of intense emotion when it had seemed appropriate to hug him, but under the present calm circumstances, I decided a curtsy was the least awkward way of greeting him. He nodded, looking pleased with the formality.

When Little Ben had filled him in on everything that had happened, Oaroboarus reached into his box of cards and pulled one out. Then he hesitated for a moment and put it back in. I had never seen him do that before. In fact, I had never seen him change his mind about *anything.*

"If you can think of anything that might be helpful," I told him, "now is not the time to censor yourself."

He sighed and nodded.

"Is he evil?" Little Ben asked.

I personally would not have considered unreliable worse than evil, but I understood why Oaroboarus did. The giant pig was the most muleheaded creature I had ever met, and

I could see him appreciating a stubbornly consistent villain over an inconsistent hero.

"Reliable or not," I said, "we need all the help we can get."

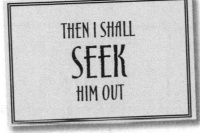

THEN I SHALL

SEEK

HIM OUT

"Can you help us get home first? I could use some clothes that haven't had dirt exploded all over them."

Oaroboarus turned to Little Ben.

DO YOU

HAVE THE—

"Shh!" Little Ben interrupted him. "I want it to be a surprise. Anyway, no, it was in my carpetbag."

I wondered what they were talking about, and I wondered even more about the dash that cut off Oaroboarus's card in midmessage. When he selected it from his box, how did he know he was going to be interrupted? I had never been able to get him to explain how he always had exactly the right cards.

FOR THE
PRESENT, I

CANNOT BE
👁 SEEN 👁
ABOVE GROUND

I CAN DELIVER
YOU BY
THE SEWERS

"Sure," I said. "It'll be like old times."

Part Two

CHAPTER 18

I stuck my head up carefully through the manhole cover, startling a woman who was pushing a baby carriage along the sidewalk. "Sorry," I said, but she didn't seem eager to accept the apology of a scraggly, stinky, dirt-covered apparition. She ran off, the wheels of her baby carriage squeaking frantically.

I had emerged across the street and down the block from the building where we lived, and as I took in the scene, I was glad we hadn't come up closer to it. A muscular man sat on our front stoop. Another stood nearby, pretending rather unconvincingly to look at a map. Two others sat on a bench, reading newspapers without ever turning the pages. I could even see one looking out our window, up on the second floor.

If their bulky physiques hadn't tipped me off, their rough orange complexions would have made it clear who they were.

"Corkers," I whispered, lowering my head partly into the manhole so that only my eyes poked about above ground. "If we try to go home, we're going right back to jail. There's only one thing to do."

Mom nodded resolutely. "Buy a new flat."

"What? No. We're going to have to find out who really stole those stones. If we can't prove we're innocent, we're going to be on the lam for the rest of our lives."

"You could live in the sewer with us," Little Ben said.

"I appreciate that, but you're wanted, too. Eventually, they'd catch all of us."

Dasra came down the front stoop of our building. The Corkers let him pass. Didn't they know he was Lady Roslyn's grandson? Well, I did. And our investigation was going to start with him.

"The Corkers haven't spotted me yet," I said, "but even at this distance, if I pop out of the ground, they're going to notice. We need a distraction."

PERMIT ME TO
ASSIST

I SHALL REUNITE
WITH YOU

AFTER I HAVE PERFORMED
CERTAIN
ERRANDS

Oaroboarus vanished down a twist of the sewer. A few moments later, the manhole cover nearest the Corkers shot upwards in a burst of sewage. They rushed over to investigate. Even the one at the window looked towards it.

"Come on!" I said, clambering out. I reached down and helped Mom and Little Ben up. We ducked around the corner, out of sight of the Corkers, and hid behind a bench.

Dasra rounded the corner. We waited for him to pass by and followed him all the way to Swiss Cottage Tube, where we got on the Tube carriage behind him.

"So why exactly are we following Dasra?" Little Ben asked as the train started.

I couldn't believe he even needed to ask that. "Because he's Lady Roslyn's spy. Why else would he live beneath us?"

"Because he and his mom moved to London to be closer to his grandma, and she's letting them stay in her flat? Remember how surprised he was to see you in jail. If he was spying on you, wouldn't he already know you were there?"

That was annoyingly rational, but I decided I didn't believe it. "He never said he was surprised to see me. He just used a surprised tone of voice and let us draw our own conclusions. I bet he learned that trick from his grandmother."

Little Ben didn't look convinced. "When you met him the first time, was he friendly and chatty? That's how I'd be if I was trying to find out what you were up to."

"No," I admitted. "But maybe he knew I'd find out who

his grandmother was, and then I'd be suspicious, and being unfriendly would be the perfect cover!"

Little Ben frowned, but the train slowed down, and he changed the subject. "How are we going to know when he gets off?"

"You'll have to peek out discreetly," I told him. "He's seen less of you. Fingers crossed he won't spot you in the crowd."

I was pretty sure crossing fingers wasn't a real magical activity, but just to be safe, I crossed them. Maybe it helped, because Little Ben managed to keep an eye out at every stop without getting caught, and when Dasra got out at Green Park, he didn't notice us trailing behind.

We kept a safe distance as he walked down the street and went into a gray stone building.

The main part of the building was tall and impressive, with high windows and bright red flags advertising the Royal Academy of Arts. The part that Dasra had entered was shorter and more modest; it looked added on as an afterthought. Instead of bright flags, there were simple brass letters next to the wooden door: SOCIETY OF GEOLOGICAL HISTORIANS.

"It's a building full of rock experts," Little Ben said. "That *is* a little suspicious."

"Lady Roslyn said if she was the thief, her next act would be to eliminate anybody with enough knowledge to catch her."

"She also said she wasn't the thief."

"She never said it wasn't her grandson."

We looked at each other.

Then we ran inside, as fast as we could.

Then I ran back outside again and yelled, "Mom! Stop gawking at the building and come inside!"

Then I ran back in again.

CHAPTER 19

$\mathscr{A}$s we burst in through the door, the receptionist looked up at us in surprise. Geological historians probably didn't get many emergency visits. I tried to look as calm as I could. "Is there anybody here who studies the link between rocks and magic?"

I was worried she'd think I was crazy, but she looked amused. "Is this for some kind of school assignment? There was a young man asking about the same thing."

"Oh, that's Dasra," Mom said. "He's—"

"We're working on the same project," I glasshoused.

"Like I told him, you want the society historian. Up the steps, first door on the left."

Little Ben and I sprinted up the steps, past busts of eminent geologists and giant geological maps of England, our feet silent on the thick carpet. At the top, we pushed open the wooden doors and hurried through.

We looked wildly around. The historian's office was narrower than a normal room but twice as tall, and ringed with a double layer of bookshelves, like a library stacked on a library. Halfway up, a wooden balcony ran around the wall, giving access to the highest stacks.

There was no sign of Dasra. The only occupant was a bespectacled, balding man, sitting behind the most remarkable desk I had ever seen. It looked like a dozen slabs of rectangular stone piled on top of each other. A stone nameplate sitting on top identified the rumpled man behind it as Jeremiah Champney, Historian of Geological Folklore.

The two of us hadn't exactly entered quietly, but the man didn't notice us; he was too absorbed in the old book he was reading.

"Mr. Champney," Little Ben said. He didn't look up, so Ben tapped him on the shoulder.

"You're in terrible danger," I told him.

His eyes opened wide. He stared at me. And he put the book down, which, based on his expression, was a tremendous sacrifice. "Danger? What sort?"

"There are powerful magic forces that—"

That was as far as I got. He interrupted me with a sigh, picked up his book, and went right back to reading it.

Little Ben and I exchanged astonished glances. "Your life is in peril!" Little Ben said.

"Yes, yes, magic forces. Thank you for warning me," he said without looking up.

I come from a family of bookworms, so I understood Mr. Champney's desire to be left alone with his book. But under the circumstances, I had no choice. I turned around and lay backwards across his desk, so that my head was on top of his book. "I'm not sure you really heard what we said."

He sighed again. "Young lady, I heard your warning perfectly well. I also heard the warning issued to me last month by the gentleman who thought the stones of St. Paul's were conspiring against the queen, as well as the woman who believed she was being followed by the cliffs of Dover, and— well, suffice it to say that over my years of research, I have personally disproven hundreds of legends regarding the alleged magical properties of rocks and gemstones."

Without waiting for an answer, he slid the book out from under my head and went back to reading it.

"But we know magic is real!" Little Ben said. "We've seen it!"

"Mmm," Mr. Champney said without looking up.

"There's a woman named Lady Roslyn—"

Mr. Champney lifted his eyes, although it was only so that he could give me a skeptical look. "Let me guess. She is a mysterious older woman. She told you there are magical forces all around you, and that you have some sort of special destiny."

"Well . . . that's true, but . . ."

"Bog-standard patter for charlatans, I'm afraid." He looked back down at his book.

That was when Mom finally wandered in. I'm not sure what she had been doing all this time, but clearly the urgency of the situation hadn't quite registered with her, because the first thing she did was admire the architecture. "The wooden bannister on the balcony is lovely," she said.

Despite myself, I looked where she was pointing. Unfortunately, the columns were about as uninteresting as I would have expected. Fortunately, as I looked, something more interesting poked out between them. Unfortunately, that thing was a weapon.

Admittedly, the weapon was a finger. But the finger was describing magical-looking motions in the air, and the tip of it glowed, and the finger's owner peered down at us with an expression of intense malice.

I grabbed a marble paperweight off Mr. Champney's desk and threw it.

It crashed into the finger just as the glow reached a crescendo. A beam of light shot out of the fingertip, but the shot went wild, hitting the curtain by the window and singeing a huge hole in it.

The curtain flew back, revealing Dasra, who must have been hiding behind it the whole time. A smoking black mark on the wall next to him showed where the bolt had hit.

"*You*," he snarled, glaring at me. He ran for the door.

I jumped up to stop him, but Little Ben pointed up to

the balcony. "She's firing again!" he yelled, and indeed, the stranger was once again pointing her glowing finger downwards.

Simultaneously, Little Ben and I leapt over the desk, knocking Mr. Champney to the floor. This time the bolt slammed into the carpet halfway between the desk and the door, which Dasra had just swung open.

Without looking back, Dasra ran out.

As I jumped to my feet to follow him, the finger-wielder shaped both hands into claws and jumped down from the balcony. Beams of light blasted from each finger, slowing her descent like jets from a rocket. She landed in front of the door, blocking my way.

CHAPTER 20

She was about my age, and she wore a long white robe, belted around her waist with a fringed red scarf. The most striking thing about her was her arms and hands. From the still-glowing tips of her fingers, all the way up to where the robe's short sleeves began, she was covered with intricately tattooed letters. Under other circumstances, I probably would have wondered why her parents let her get full-arm tattoos when I wasn't even allowed to get my ears pierced, but at the moment, I was a little more concerned with the whole trying-to-stop-her-from-killing-someone thing.

Little Ben and I slid together, blocking her access to Mr. Champney. If she wanted to blast him, she'd have to go through us.

She glared at me, and a handful of tattooed letters

rearranged themselves, lighting up as if aflame. I'm not going to repeat the words they spelled, but trust me: they were not nice ones.

She must have decided we weren't worth it. She spun around and ran out.

Little Ben and I chased after her.

Out in the hallway, she leapt over the banister and did the finger-rocket float down the stairwell. We had to use our feet on the steps, which was slower. By the time we got down, she was already out the front door. And by the time we got out the front door, she and Dasra had vanished into the throng of shoppers that mobbed Piccadilly.

With no clue as to the direction they'd gone in, there was no point in trying to find them again. Anyway, I knew where Dasra lived. "Let's see if Mr. Champney believes in magic *now*," I told Little Ben.

As we reentered his office, Mom was in midmonologue. "My sister Mel was always fond of rocks," she was saying, "and she had the most lovely collection of— Oh, hello, dear. Mr. Champney was very interested in my family. I feel like I've known him for years!"

Mr. Champney nodded politely. "Yes, madam, it was all fascinating. Now, if you'll excuse me." He turned to me. "How did that girl—what was—how did—" He paused and pulled himself together. "I tried to call the police," he finally said. "But I couldn't describe what I saw without sounding like a madman, so I hung up."

I was glad. The last thing I wanted was for the police

to find us again—let alone at the scene of another crime. I decided not to mention that to Mr. Champney. "We don't think you're crazy," I told him. "The problem is, neither does Lady Roslyn."

Little Ben cleared his throat. "Or whoever is behind this."

I stared at him in amazement. "Have you been here the whole time? You can draw a direct line from Lady Roslyn to that tattoo girl, and the line's name is Dasra."

"I know. It's totally suspicious! I'm just saying we need more evidence before we jump to any conclusions."

I turned back to Mr. Champney. "One thing we know for sure is that somebody just tried to kill you. And we're pretty sure it's because of something you know."

"All I know is folklore and myth. Why would anybody want to kill me over that?"

"Maybe some of your myths happen to be true."

"That girl did remind me of something I've read," Mr. Champney muttered, his eyes beginning to glaze over. I recognized that look. In Aunt Topsy, it always came right before she went hunting for something in a book.

Sure enough, he stood up and ran his fingers along one of the lower shelves. "Here it is. Mayhew's *Oral History of London Stonemasons*." He flipped through it, found the right page, and began to read. " 'Used though they are to hard work, stone carvers dream of an easier method of plying their task. A legend among them tells of a young woman named Minnie Tickle, daughter of a scholar known only as the

Precious Man. The Precious Man learned ancient words of power, which he inscribed upon her arms, granting her the ability to cut the hardest masonry with her bare fingers.'"

He lowered the book onto the table so that we could see the illustration. It was a young woman in a long white robe, belted with a fringed red scarf. Tattooed letters ran up and down her arms.

"That's her!" Little Ben gasped.

"Unlikely, as the book was published one hundred fifty years ago." Mr. Champney stood up from his desk and began to pace, talking more to himself than to us. "It's certainly the same costume. Is it possible that the legend was true? It seems so unlikely. Surely others have read this book and seen this illustration. Surely anyone could get a robe and tattoos. And that light—it could have been a laser, or some sort of Roman candle up her sleeve. Yes, that sounds much more sensible. No need to invoke the extraordinary to explain the commonplace."

I sighed. He hadn't merely *seen* magic—he had almost been murdered by it. But in the space of about ten seconds, he had managed to convince himself that nothing unusual had happened. I was beginning to understand how the government could station creatures made out of living cork on a public street without making the evening news.

"However you explain it, she was trying to kill you," I told Mr. Champney. "Promise me you'll be careful."

"I will," he said. Then a thought occurred to him, and for the first time, I felt like he was looking directly at Little Ben and me, instead of seeing us through a fog of history books. "And you, young lady, and you, young man: promise me you won't pursue this any further."

Little Ben shook his head. "No way!"

"I can't promise that," I said.

"You must. She is dangerous, and you are young." His focus shifted, as if he was once again peering into his memories, and he added, more softly, "No parent should ever have to contemplate losing their child."

"All the more reason for us to go after her," I said. "She's no older than I am, and she's mixed up in something dangerous. We'll stop her—for her own good."

"If her father is deluded enough to think he's this 'Precious Man,' then he is even more dangerous than she is. Who knows how far he would go? But I can see I'm not convincing you. Whether or not this is genuine magic, I may know something that could save your life. Promise me, then, that you will report back to me, and let me advise you."

"Now *that* is a promise I can make," I said.

"Me too!" Little Ben said.

"Me too," Mom said. "It's like Grandma always says: *It's always good to give your word, when historical facts you've recently heard.*"

I could see Mr. Champney struggling to make sense of that, but after a few seconds, he shook his head as if to clear it and opened the book up again. "In that case, you may be interested in the next passage. 'A particularly aged stonemason was prevailed on to recite the following bit of doggerel:

" 'Where 13 Park Lane stands by 13 The Mall,
The Precious Man comes to answer the call.
Where 13 Downing Street meets 13 The Strand,
The Precious Man takes the book in his hand.
Where 13 Fen Court meets 13 Sutton Walk,
The Precious Man proves he's as sharp as a hawk.' "

Mr. Champney stopped. We waited for him to continue, but he closed the book. "That, I'm afraid, is all the help this book offers."

"But what does it mean?" Little Ben asked. "The Precious Man is looking for a book?"

"*Was* looking," Mr. Champney corrected me. "Remember, this describes the historical Precious Man—although *historical* may not be the right word for a such a mythical-sounding figure."

"But if somebody is going to the trouble of dressing up like the Precious Man's daughter, and discovering his words of power," I said, "it seems pretty likely they're trying to follow the same path he did. And if we can figure out what path that is, we're one step closer to catching him—and clearing our name."

CHAPTER 21

We all agreed: 13 Park Lane, 13 Fen Court—they had to be addresses. Well, Little Ben and I agreed. Mom thought it might be an actual lane with thirteen parks, or an actual court with thirteen fens. But we convinced her to check out the addresses first.

When we got to Park Lane, Mom gave a confused frown. (Side note: you might imagine that Mom always looked confused, but you'd be wrong. Whatever idea was in her head at any given moment, Mom believed it with complete self-assurance. It's those of us around her who felt confused.)

"I don't think there is a number thirteen," Mom told me.

"I hardly think a whole building just vanished," I said. But it turns out that was *exactly* what had happened.

At the bottom end of the street was 1 Park Lane, the

InterContinental Hotel. The next building you came to was 22 Park Lane. In between was a long wall of grayish-white stone, as blank as if something had once been there but had gotten erased.

It was the same story on the Strand. There was a nondescript office building at number 11, and a noodle restaurant at number 32. In between was Charing Cross station, where we spent half an hour wandering around, trying to find somebody who could tell us the street number. Everybody we asked insisted it didn't have one. "It's just Charing Cross station, The Strand, London," said the man at the information desk.

And the Mall? Not only were there no street numbers, there were almost no buildings. The only one we could find was the Institute of Contemporary Arts. I don't know which arts they considered contemporary, but apparently Having a Sensible Address wasn't one of them, because when we went inside and asked to know the street number, we got the same runaround we had gotten at Charing Cross. I thought about staging a sit-in and refusing to leave until we got an answer, but then I noticed the security guards looking at us as if they recognized us. Would Brigadier Beale have distributed our photo to non-magical, non-cork security forces? I decided we shouldn't stick around long enough to find out.

As we wandered from one nonexistent address to another, I started paying attention to the street numbers I did see, and they made no sense whatsoever. Sometimes the odd numbers were on one side of the street and the even numbers on the other, and sometimes they weren't. Sometimes the numbers on one side of the street counted up while the numbers on the other side counted down. Sometimes the numbers jumped around with no pattern whatsoever.

And just to make it more fun, most buildings didn't display any numbers at all.

I thought of something Little Ben had once told me: *Ninety percent of British life makes total sense. The other ten percent seems absolutely bonkers, if you don't know about the secret rivers. So if you're trying to find magic, it's that ten percent you have to pay attention to.*

It was certainly crazy to assign street numbers with the gleeful abandon of a preschooler flinging paint, and then not even bother to display them. Was it all just an elaborate ruse to hide the fact that number 13 was missing from so many streets?

If it *was* all a plot to keep us from finding number 13, there were some streets where they had taken even greater precautions. We couldn't get close to the building that should have been 13 Downing Street, because the entire street was blocked by a huge fence, which in turn was guarded by machine-gun-toting soldiers. Admittedly, the block also contained 10 Downing Street, which is where the prime minister lives, so the guards could have had something to do with that.

We had one last hope: 13 Sutton Walk. Sutton Walk was a short path under a railway bridge, with no buildings at all. The rumbling of trains made it difficult to hear each other, so we crossed the street to a row of stone benches and sat down to talk.

"Is it superstition?" Little Ben asked. "The number thirteen is supposed to be bad luck. Maybe they just skip the number because nobody wants to live at Thirteen Whatever Street."

"Then why do they work so hard to hide it?" I asked. "It ought to be a selling point. 'Come to London! Number Thirteen—free since 1653!'"

The sun was setting on a long day, full of mysteries that had only multiplied the more we had investigated them. Also, I was still wearing the same clothes I had slid down a collapsing dirt hole in. I wanted answers and I wanted a shower and I would have been happy with them in either order, or maybe both at once.

"Psst!" a voice rumbled, interrupting my thoughts.

I looked in surprise at Little Ben, and he looked at me, and we both looked at my mom. None of us had done the psst-ing.

"Psst!" the voice rumbled again, and this time, we all looked behind us. The benches sat in front of an iron fence with a stone base, and on the other side of it, a massive stone lion was crouched, out of sight of the passersby.

"I say, you there—Hyacinth, is it?" whispered the lion, as quietly as a massive stone lion could whisper. "Oaroboarus asked me to look you, you, you up. My colleagues and I might have some, some, some useful intelligence in aid of your quest."

CHAPTER 22

"*I* know you!" I exclaimed. On my previous adventure with Lady Roslyn, I had been locked up in the medium-security division of the Mount Pleasant Mail Sorting Facility, along with a roomful of terrifying magical creatures. The giant stone lion was the only one who had been kind to me— although I hadn't exactly repaid his kindness. "I'm sorry about the whole sending-you-flying-into-a-unicorn thing," I told him.

"NONSENSE!" he roared, causing a number of passersby to look over in shock. He ducked back out of sight and tried to speak quietly. "Delighted to have helped. Only sorry I couldn't have taken a, taken a more active, if you will, active role in the rescue that you, that you so bravely and autonomously initiated."

His speech poured out in an energetic rush, and when he stammered, it was as if multiple words were trying to get through the door at once and ended up blocking each other's way. Even so, he talked much more coherently than he had when I'd seen him in jail, and I thought I knew why. "You seem a lot more . . . sober," I told him.

"Yes, yes, thankfully. Very embarrassed about the, the state you saw me in. I've, I've, I've turned over an entirely new leaf, I can, I can assure you."

"Mom, Little Ben, this is . . . Actually, I don't think I ever got your name."

"HUNGERFORD!" he roared again, then cleared his throat and went back to his previous loud whisper. "At your, at your, delighted to be at your service."

He turned around and began crawling along the ground at the foot of the fence, in an apparent effort to stay out of sight. Of course, with his big stone head sticking up above the wall and his voice constantly booming up to a roar before he remembered to lower it to a slightly quieter whisper, he was not exactly inconspicuous.

We hurried along on our side of the fence as he kept up his monologue. "It's, it's, it's fortunate that my path has re-connected with yours, allowing me to demonstrate my, my more typical reliability, and to correct the earlier unfortunate impression you must have received of, of, of me."

As he talked, he walked along one side of the yard and turned right. Still on the other side of the fence, we did our best to keep up.

At the next corner, the fence intersected a tall glass entry-way with a staircase inside. We opened a door from our side and stepped in as he jumped into it through a window on his side. While he was in midair, I managed to get a word in edgewise. "You said something about having colleagues?"

He landed and trotted briskly down the stairs. "Yes, yes, yes, fellow products of Mrs. Eleanor Coade, all of us. Normally we don't, don't meet up, stationed as we are at our, our various districts and outposts, but in times of crisis, needs must, eh? Needs must."

The stairs led into a white corridor, lit by glowing red lights high in the wall. Hungerford walked with a brisk, bouncy, slightly clumsy stride, as if he had too much energy to focus on a little thing like forward movement.

The corridor turned, and we found ourselves in a space unlike any I'd been in. Hallways and stairs spilled in all directions, including directions that stairs and hallways shouldn't go in. Windows in hallways going sideways looked out onto hallways going simultaneously up and down past staircases that were somehow diagonal to themselves. And if you don't think that makes sense to read, you should try looking at it.

My stomach lurched. Mom turned green. Little Ben broke into a huge smile. "Cool!" he said. "It's like being in an Escher print!"

I'm pretty sure I could have come up with a snappy answer to that, but I didn't dare open my mouth for fear that the last thing I'd eaten would come tumbling out.

"My apologies!" roared Hungerford. Now that we were

out of earshot of the crowds, he wasn't even trying to whisper. "The Coadeway is a thoroughfare for the, the convenience of the city's stone guardians, who tend to have iron stomachs, if you will forgive the mixed metaphor."

We turned left, and then right, and then up, and then in a direction that I had never encountered before. I'd describe it as 45 percent right, 78 percent left, and 100 percent queasy, and, no, that doesn't add up. If it bothers you, take it up with the intersection.

Finally, Hungerford pushed aside a large sheet of green plastic hanging over a doorway, and we stepped through into a hallway that, at long last, was made out of straight lines and ordinary right angles. On this side of the plastic sheet, a sign said DO NOT ENTER: CONSTRUCTION IN PROGRESS, probably because if it said VIOLATION OF LAWS OF GEOMETRY IN PROGRESS, people might be tempted to go in.

In front of us, a large window looked out onto a room full of musical instruments, ornately carved out of wood and painted red and gold. I didn't recognize them, but Little Ben did. "It's the Gamelan Room! We're in the Royal Festival Hall."

It took me a minute to place the name. "Isn't that the big white building we could see from those stone benches?" I turned to Hungerford. "You led us through the pedestrian equivalent of a triple-loop roller coaster, when we could have just crossed the street and gone in the front door?"

"No, no, no, to the contrary. As a magical creature, I'm, I'm, I'm forbidden to wander the streets except in case of masonry theft or other extremity. But, but, but now that you mention it, I suppose you could have walked over and met me here. APOLOGIES! Trot in haste, repent at leisure, that's what, what, what Mrs. Coade kept telling me."

He barged into the room of instruments. "You keep mentioning Mrs. Coade," I said. "Who is she?"

"She, she, she built the factory, of course."

"Which factory?"

"This one." With his large stone paw, Hungerford tapped out a tune on a nearby gamelan. For a moment, I thought I recognized it, somewhere deep in the back of my memory. Was it another family lullaby? Before I could place it, the entire wall of the room swung open, which was distracting enough to chase away the vague memory. Hungerford bounded through the newly opened gap, and with a quick glance at each other, Mom, Little Ben, and I bounded after him.

CHAPTER 23

We gasped.

The massive room was filled with living stone sculptures of every shape and size. Sitting on the wooden ceiling beams, crammed into alcoves in the walls, perched on the giant beehive-shaped brick kilns that dotted the floor, they were all talking at once. Stone cupids bickered with stone horses. A gigantic stone Egyptian god was leaning down to yell at a little stone mouse. A matched set of stone columns, each with a female head at the top, was arguing with a stone William Shakespeare. At the far end of the room, a wide stream of water ran through a channel, and stone dolphins and stone fish swam in circles around each other, sending up furious streams of bubbles.

"Silence!" roared Hungerford, and every stone head in the

room turned to look at us. The quiet only lasted a moment, before a stone sheep bleated "Humans! Hide!" and the scene turned even more chaotic, with dozens of statues running into each other in their desperation to get out of our sight.

"Move it, buster!" yelled a cupid.

"🦅 𓀭 𓇳 𓈗 𓃀," yelled the Egyptian god.

Shakespeare, meanwhile, was trying to cram himself into a tiny gap between two kilns. "Oh, that this too, too solid flesh would melt!" he intoned.

"SILENCE!" roared Hungerford, even louder than before, and everybody froze. "The human girl was with me when I was, was, was— She's seen me on a premises comprising part of the system of justice!"

A stone judge pounded his gavel on a nearby brick wall, sending up a cloud of red dust. "On your evidence, this court finds that she and her party may be present at a gathering of magical creatures."

This seemed to satisfy the statues, who finally settled down. "What is this place?" I asked Hungerford.

Little Ben answered for him. "It's the Coade stone factory," he said, looking around eagerly.

"I thought the place where stones were made was called the earth's core."

"Natural stone, sure. But in 1769, a Londoner named Eleanor Coade invented a method of making artificial stone and turning it into sculptures. When she died, her secret method was lost, and they tore down the factory and built the Royal Festival Hall over it. Or so they said."

"As you can see, there are, are, are certain crucial omissions from the public record," Hungerford said. "The factory was built above the, the Neckinger, one of the city's secret magical rivers, and the waters form a, a, a crucial part of our mixture. As a result, we're more, we're more lively than stone made with the traditional method involving magma and millennia."

"Thus, in Our royal wisdom, We ordered Coade stones posted around the city, to serve as guardians of their mundane brethren," piped up a miniature King George III, with as much dignity as a squeaky-voiced one-foot-tall statue could muster.

I probably should have addressed him as Your Majesty or something, but, look, I was raised in America. I didn't care if King George III was tiny and made out of synthetic marble—he was still my ancestral enemy. Somewhere in the world there might have been a tiny stone George Washington, and I didn't want him to feel betrayed. So instead of addressing the mini-king by title, I just pointed at him. "You've all met up here because of the stolen amphitheater."

"Not just that," whinnied a stone horse. "The crumbled walls of Merton Priory lay preserved under a Tube stop for five hundred years. Just this afternoon, someone sheared them clean off."

Other statues joined in. "Queen Caroline's bathhouse! Snatched!" called a naval captain.

"The Saxon archway from the Church of All Hallows!" honked a swan.

"Gone! Gone! All gone!" they cried. The statues that had hands beat them against their heads. The ones without hands beat their heads against the wall.

"Quiet! Please! Calm down, everyone!" I yelled.

Things settled down for a minute, until Mom couldn't contain herself anymore. "Gone!" she moaned, tears running down her face, and chaos erupted once more.

Between Hungerford's roars, and me and Little Ben yelling, we finally got everybody's attention. "You should be ashamed of yourselves," I told the stones. "Did Mrs. Coade create you to panic at the first sign of trouble? Is that why you were entrusted with the care of this ancient city's stones by his glorious majesty King George the Third?"

Yes, I know what I just said about calling him by his title, but I thought the statues needed all the bucking up they could get. Sorry, tiny stone George Washington, wherever you are.

In fact, I had probably laid it on too thick, because the naval captain waved his stone hat in the air, calling "God save the king!" and it took another minute or two before the cheering stopped. When it did, I got right to the point. "We need to focus on catching the thieves. Did any of you see them?"

"It was a girl with tattoos," said a massive stone child. "She stole the walls of St. Dunstan in the East."

"Aye," said the captain, "I saw those tattoos. Nice work, they was."

The other statues nodded. "It was her! We saw her!" they called.

"Did any of you see where she went?"

The Coade stones that had necks all hung their heads. The others looked necklessly sheepish.

"That's okay," I said quickly, hoping to forestall another mass panic. "We just have to figure out where she's going to strike next. Everything she's taken has been the remnant of some ancient structure. Are any of those still left?"

"Only one," said a stone angel, accompanying herself on a stone harp. "She hasn't gotten the section of Roman wall that's in the car park near the Barbican."

"Well then," I said, "I know where we're camping out tonight."

CHAPTER 24

*O*ther than the name, the London Wall car park didn't seem all that special. For a few hundred feet from the entrance, it was a regular garage, lit by fluorescent lights, with numbered spaces along both walls. I was glad to see that there were more handicapped spaces than usual—Aunt Talia used a wheelchair, and I had many memories of circling a parking lot with her, trying to find a space.

It was only when we got to the rear of the garage that things got strange. Sprawling across several spaces was a section of Roman wall, about twice as tall as I was, made mostly of gray stone with a few lines of red brick.

Looking at it sticking up between a station wagon and a gaggle of motorcycles, I didn't need Little Ben to tell me that it was part of the magic 10 percent.

Nearby was a door marked STRICTLY NO ENTRY. It swung open and Oaroboarus squeezed his bulk through the doorway. In his mouth, he had a carpetbag that looked exactly like the one Brigadier Beale had confiscated. He handed it to Little Ben, then bowed his head courteously.

Hungerford had insisted that we go in first while he checked "the, the perimeter." Now a wave of car alarms, getting closer and closer, announced that he had returned. He was creeping along close to the wall, trying to hide, but he kept bumping his giant stone rump against cars.

Finally, he arrived, knocking over a handful of motorcycles as he did so. That was when he spotted Oaroboarus. Hungerford rushed up and threw his big paws in the air as if he was about to hug Oaroboarus, but when he was an inch away, he finally noticed the giant pig's unfriendly glare.

Hungerford tried to turn the almost-hug into a stretch and ended up tumbling over himself onto the floor. "Oaroboarus," he said, looking up at the pig. "It's lovely, lovely to see you. You're looking very, very, very fine."

Oaroboarus nodded grudgingly and threw down a single card.

HUNGERFORD.

Our party found a nook about twenty feet away from the Roman wall, behind yet another set of handicapped parking spaces, and settled down for the night.

If you've never camped out in an underground garage, I highly recommend it. The smell of tires and gas isn't quite as lovely as the scent of pine, and the sound of traffic rumbling overhead isn't as soothing as crickets, but you get used to them after a while. And it's nice to have a roof over your head and walls to protect you from the rain. Plus, although we couldn't start a fire, there was a twenty-four-hour coffee shop two blocks away, so we had plenty of hot chocolate to keep warm.

Finally, I could barely keep my eyes open. Mom was in the middle of an endless anecdote that I think had to do with my grandfather and a tree, but I found Mom's stories hard enough to track when I was fully alert. Oaroboarus noticed that I was beginning to slump over.

PERHAPS WE SHOULD

SLEEP IN SHIFTS

I WILL TAKE THE FIRST WATCH

I didn't need to be asked twice, and neither did Little Ben. He fluffed up his carpetbag and we lay down next to each other, using it as a pillow.

"So do you have a stash of those bags somewhere?" I asked. "Or did Oaroboarus somehow get it back from Beale?"

"Neither!" Little Ben said. "There's a little corner in the sewer near where I live. Whenever I lose my bag, another one appears there. And anything that was in the old bag is in the new one."

"Maybe it's the same bag, finding its way home."

"That's what I thought, but then I accidentally burned

my bag doing an experiment, and it somehow turned up again in the usual spot, good as new. It's a mystery!"

As I contemplated that, my eyes drifted shut.

Next thing I knew, Mom was tapping us awake. She put her finger to her lips and pointed back towards the Roman wall.

"She's here," Mom whispered.

CHAPTER 25

A figure in a short-sleeved white robe, with a red scarf tied around the waist, stood by the Roman wall, her back to us. If her costume hadn't told me who she was, the swirling letters on her arm would have.

The letters coalesced into words. From the distance, I couldn't make them out, but they must have been powerful, because they began to shine brightly, their glow starting up by her shoulder and racing down to her wrist. As it did, she lifted her hand and pointed at the wall, and when the glow reached her finger, it shot out, making a bright line on the stones.

She wrote with her fingertip, in letters of fire. Unlike the words on her arm, I could read these from a distance because they were two feet tall and also, you know, *fire*. They said *Mene, mene, tekel, upharsin.*

Hey, I said I could read them. I never said I could understand them.

But Little Ben seemed to know what they meant. His jaw dropped. He caught my glance and mouthed *Tell you later.* I nodded.

The girl added one last thing to her magical graffiti: a straight line under the words. At first, I thought it was just for emphasis, as if the two-foot-tall flaming letters weren't emphatic enough. Then it burned out, leaving behind a perfectly straight fracture all along the length of the wall.

The stones toppled towards her.

The letters on her arm swiftly swirled into a new configuration, and their fiery red glow changed to a cool blue one, which raced down her arm and burst out of her fingers, enveloping the falling stones. They stopped in midair.

I had been so engrossed in what she was doing that I hadn't noticed a large van backing up to her. Now it came to a stop. She strode over to it, and with the hand that wasn't pointing at the floating stones, she swung open the rear door. She gestured with both hands, as if inviting the cut wall into the van, and it floated inside.

She slammed the van door, and as it drove off, she hopped onto a nearby motorcycle and revved it up.

Wait, tattoos *and* a motorcycle? The Precious Man might have been a nefarious heritage-stealing villain, but he was also the coolest dad *ever*.

Minnie took off, heading out a different exit from the van.

"We've got to split up and follow them both," I said. "One of them will lead us to the stolen stones."

"I'll follow the, the, the van," Hungerford said.

I looked at his massive form. "Can you do it without being spotted?"

"You have my, my, my most solemn word. I shall apply the, the full range of camouflage techniques available to a sophisticated jungle predator."

He bounded off and crashed into a car, denting its side and setting off its alarm. After a moment of staggering, he righted himself and dashed away.

"We'll follow her," I said. "Oaroboarus, can you give us a ride?"

Mom looked up at him. "Is he . . . I mean, are you safe?"

Oaroboarus reached into his pouch and pulled out a different kind of card—laminated, with his photo on it.

TRANSPORT FOR LONDON
MAGICAL BEING PASSENGER
LICENSE NUMBER 864302
Name: Oaroboarus
Licensed to carry up to 3 passengers

Notes & Restrictions: Disguise required when in non-magical realm

"We got it after our last adventure," Little Ben said. "We didn't want Oaroboarus to risk getting arrested. Ooh, that reminds me. Look what else we have!"

He reached into his carpetbag and pulled out a thick bundle of cloth and metal. He put it onto Oaroboarus's back, and when Oaroboarus shook himself, the bundle unfolded into a double-decker bus costume.

"We made it ourselves, out of stuff that washed down the sewer," Little Ben added, although I could have guessed. It was a mishmash of elements and a dozen different shades of red. One of the wheels was from a horse cart, and another was from a bicycle, and none of them were the same size. The "driver" was a stuffed toy gorilla wearing a Prince Charles mask. Plus, although Oaroboarus was huge for a pig, he was awfully small for a bus. Still, I couldn't fault their attention to detail. They had even put an ad on the side, made from whatever fragments they could find:

DR. CLARET'S EFFERVESCENT BRAIN SALTS.
NOW WITH A FIVE-MEGAPIXEL TV DINNER.
Groovy!

Little Ben was looking at me with his usual eagerness, waiting for me to say something. I didn't want to tell the truth and hurt his feelings, but I also didn't want to lie and make things blow up. "It's unbelievable!" I blurted ambiguously. Then, before he had time to figure out whether or not that was a compliment, I climbed on board. "Let's go!"

"You're not going anywhere until you give us back the stones," a voice boomed.

Brigadier Beale stood between us and the exit Minnie had used, dozens of Corkers behind him. From the opposite side, more Corkers poured in, blocking the only other exit.

CHAPTER 26

The megaphone in Beale's hand kind of seemed like overkill—he wasn't more than ten feet away from us. Still, the ringing that his overamplified voice left in my ears was the least of my problems. "This isn't how it looks," I said, pointing at the freshly cut wall. "Unless it looks like somebody else stole it and we're about to catch her."

"Present arms!" Brigadier Beale boomed. Behind him, the front row of Corkers raised their guns. These guns weren't like any I had seen before—they had the big round cartridges of a gangster's tommy gun, but in place of a gun barrel, there was a large slingshot.

"Put up your hands, get off the pig, and walk slowly forwards," Beale said.

"Let me make a counteroffer," I said. "We're leaving,

and if your men don't get out of our way, Oaroboarus is going to knock them all down."

Picking up my cue, Oaroboarus trotted forwards menacingly.

"Warning shot," Beale called. The Corker closest to him pointed his weapon at Oaroboarus's feet and pulled the trigger. Gunfire raked the ground, forcing Oaroboarus to stop.

Then one of the bullets bounced up in the air and landed on my lap, and I realized it wasn't gunfire at all. They were shooting pebbles at us.

I didn't have much time to wonder about it, though. "Stop her!" Beale yelled. The Corkers stood shoulder to shoulder and began to swell, until both exits had been filled by an impenetrable mass of uniformed orangey skin.

"Did he say 'stop her' or 'stopper'?" Mom asked.

"Ooh, good question," Little Ben said.

I was about to be annoyed with them for getting distracted when I realized that Mom might have somehow hit on something. He *had* said "stopper"—and it wasn't the first time I had heard the word used as a verb.

Once, a bunch of my aunts got together for a big winemaking project. But when they stoppered the bottles—that is, when they put the corks in them—they had done something wrong.

A few weeks later, we were in the basement to check on them and the corks all popped out. As we dodged the flying corks, we slipped on spilled wine, and we all ended up flat on the floor, laughing. Afterwards, Aunt Rainey explained what had happened. "As the wine fermented," she said, "air pressure built up inside the bottles, and eventually, it forced the corks out."

So I knew what stoppering was—and I knew that you could pop corks out from the inside, if you put steady pressure on them. I leaned over and whispered in Oaroboarus's ear. "This is going to seem crazy, but trust me." Then I sat up and pointed at Brigadier Beale. "ATTACK!" I yelled.

Oaroboarus charged. As the massive pig bounded towards him, Brigadier Beale's eyes widened, but he didn't blanch. "Fire!" he yelled.

"Reverse!" I told Oaroboarus. "Head for the other exit."

Surprisingly nimble for such a giant creature, Oaroboarus pirouetted, dodging a hailstorm of pebblefire, and ran back towards the other side of the garage. That way was blocked by Corkers, too, of course—but that was part of my plan.

"Keep running back and forth in front of them," I told Oaroboarus. As he did so, I ducked down, and Mom and Little Ben did the same, while pebbles pocked and pinged off the metal plates of the bus costume.

More importantly, they pocked and pinged off the wall of Corkers. I stuck my head up long enough to see that the pebbly onslaught was slowly pushing them back. "Keep going!" I called to Oaroboarus.

The Corkers moved back a little more . . . a little more . . . a little more . . . and then all at once, they exploded backwards, flying out of the garage and into the street beyond.

As pebbles pinged behind us, Oaroboarus sprinted through the newly opened exit. The Corkers beyond were already bouncing back up, but now that they were separated, Oaroboarus barreled through them easily.

Little Ben pointed up at the sky. "Wow! They've got a helicopter!" he said.

He was right. The chopper hung in the sky, firing pebbles downwards at something several blocks away from us.

"I bet it's chasing Minnie," I said. "Follow that helicopter."

While Oaroboarus ran towards it, I pulled the pebble out of my pocket and held it up. "They're not using regular ammo," I said.

"That's good," Little Ben said as Oaroboarus swerved

to avoid running over a group of toddlers crossing the street. "Otherwise, this could be dangerous."

By now, we were in sight of Minnie, who was weaving wildly through traffic while the helicopter sprayed pebbles at her. The streets were full of cars, honking as they dodged Minnie, and the sidewalks were full of people, screaming and dropping their lunches as they dodged the pebblefire.

"I can see why Inspector Sands said the Corkers were unsafe for bystanders," I said, and then another thought occurred to me. "Hey, remember what else Inspector Sands said? About what stones do?"

"Ooh, yes! They absorb magic. You think they're trying to turn off her powers?"

"That's my guess."

Minnie's tattoos were swirling once more. Keeping one hand on her handlebars, she lifted the other and pointed a finger towards the helicopter. Her hand glowed a fiery red— but then a pebble hit it, and the flow fizzled out immediately.

By now, traffic had come to a complete standstill. Minnie zipped between two rows of stopped cars and vanished around a corner.

Oaroboarus's eyes narrowed into a familiar look of stubborn determination, and I knew he was not going to let her get away. He jumped up onto a car and began to hop from roof to roof in a highly un-buslike way. Then he leapt off onto the sidewalk, skidded around the corner, and squeezed through a row of trash cans, and we found ourselves on London Bridge.

Mom and I had seen London Bridge in our first few days in the UK, and I had found it pretty disappointing. It was an ordinary, not-very-attractive bridge. But now, as we got closer and closer to Minnie, I finally found something to appreciate about it: it had a lovely sidewalk, just wide enough for a giant pig in a bus costume.

CHAPTER 28

$\mathcal{A}$s we galloped off the bridge into a short tunnel under a railway, we finally caught up with Minnie's motorcycle. It was parked next to a pedestrian passage leading off to one side. The only problem was, she wasn't on it.

"Ooh, smart," Little Ben said. "She got off under the railway tracks, out of view of the helicopter."

"Let's steal her idea," I said. "Oaroboarus, let me and Little Ben climb down. Then you keep going. I bet the helicopter is tracking us as well—let them see you come out of the tunnel."

Mom started to climb down with us. The next bit was going to require some subtlety and good judgment, which were not qualities I thought Mom particularly possessed. So I quickly added, "Mom, you'd better stay with Oaroboarus.

We . . . um . . . we might need him in a hurry, and we can't wait for a message to work its way through the sewer system. Stay close and be ready to answer your phone."

The pedestrian passage was made of arched brown brick, thick enough to block out the sound of gunfire and the helicopter, and there was no sign here of the panic we had seen on the street outside. Instead, a meandering mob strolled in both directions. We pushed our way through.

The passage opened up into a broad market square, with stalls selling all kinds of food under a wide awning that said BOROUGH MARKET. As the smells wafted by, I realized I hadn't eaten anything since last night. I turned to Little Ben. "You know what the problem with magical adventures is? Not enough lunch breaks."

"When we catch Minnie, we'll make her cook us hot dogs with her fingers," he said.

"Speaking of flaming fingers, you seemed to recognize the words she was writing," I said.

"Oh, yeah! They're from the Bible. The book of Daniel, chapter five. King Belshazzar of Babylon threw a feast, and in the middle of it, a disembodied hand appeared. With its finger, it wrote a mysterious message on the wall: *mene, mene, tekel, upharsin.*"

"The same words Minnie wrote. But what do they mean?"

"*You've been weighed in the balance and found wanting, and your kingdom will be divided.*"

"That doesn't sound good."

"It wasn't. The king was killed that night, and his kingdom was broken up."

"Is there anything in the story about the Precious Man?"

Little Ben shook his head. "Not that I remember."

"Wait!" I said. "Remember that book that Mr. Champney read us? It said the Precious Man's daughter was named Minnie Tickle. But it was an oral history. I bet the stone carver said *Mene Tekel* and the author misheard."

"Ooh, I bet you're right!"

"I'm going to stick with 'Minnie Tickle,'" I said. "She's kind of intimidating. I'm hoping a silly name will help."

We made our way past a stall selling noodles fragrant with sesame oil, and another one overflowing with fresh-baked bread. There were mushrooms sautéing in a pan as big as a wagon wheel, and—

Look at the people, Hyacinth, not the food.

I searched the faces around me. None of them were Minnie—and any of them could have been the Precious Man.

We came to a small road that ran through the middle of the market. Parked along it were delivery vehicles, and trash cans, and forklifts . . . and one familiar white van.

Little Ben spotted it, too. "There's nobody in the driver's seat. He must have met her here."

"PSST!" a voice whispered. "Over, over here."

We followed the sound to a mound of trash bags with a large stone snout sticking out. Hungerford lifted his head, sending the bags above cascading downwards. "I stuck close to, to, to my prey. Alas, I didn't get a, a, a good look at the driver when he parked and exited here, but I've staked out this, this vantage point, and I'll spot him when he returns."

"Well done!" I said.

"In, in, in my humble opinion, it was nothing out of the ordinary. But if you, if you happen to think it was a spectacularly impressive display of hunting instincts, would you mind mentioning it to Oaroboarus?"

"Sure," I said. "I'll— Hey! Over there."

Across the road, two tall green cast-iron pillars led into a roofed part of the market. And between them—was that a flash of red scarf, tied around someone's waist? "Keep an eye out here," I told Hungerford as Little Ben and I headed for the pillars.

We pushed our way through the workers in office attire and tourists in T-shirts, catching an occasional glimpse of red fabric through gaps in the mob. Suddenly, the crowd opened up, and there was Minnie, queued up at a stall selling sizzling-hot sausages.

"Should we grab her?" Little Ben whispered.

"Even if we turned her over to Brigadier Beale, he'd say we were trying to keep the stolen stones for ourselves. Until we get them back, we'll never prove we're innocent." I pulled him into the nearest queue. "Look inconspicuous," I said.

We waited there, turning our backs whenever it looked like she was about to glance over our way. She moved forwards in her queue; we moved forwards in ours.

Finally, she reached the front and whispered something

to the sausage man. He nodded. She gave him a handful of change.

"Can I help you, miss?" someone said to me. Surprised, Little Ben and I turned our attention away from Minnie and discovered we were at the front of our queue.

"Um, I'll take one, please," I said, looking back at Minnie. She was already walking away from the sausage stand—but she wasn't holding a sausage. What had she bought there?

The vendor at our stall handed me a cup of something, with a fork sticking out. "That'll be—"

"Here," I said, grabbing a bill from my pocket. "Keep the change."

Little Ben and I hurried after Minnie. "Did you see what she bought?" I asked him.

"No!" he said. "I was hoping you did!"

So far, I thought I had handled our investigation pretty well. Taking our eyes off Minnie had been my first big mistake. I was so determined not to repeat that mistake that I made a different one:

I ate what was in the cup I had bought without checking to see what it was.

And what it was, was a jellied eel.

Jellied eels, it turns out, taste like a delicious piece of delicate cooked fish, soaked in fresh snot.

"Blhrmmmmmh," I said, which is the sound of somebody who wants to shout in disgust but has to keep her mouth shut so she doesn't give herself away to the person she's tailing.

Up ahead, Minnie had made it to the van. She unlocked the back, revealing a large wheeled suitcase. For a moment, she pointed her finger at it, as if she was about to magic it down to the sidewalk. Then, remembering she was in a crowded place being hunted by soldiers, she heaved it out the old-fashioned way. It crashed onto the ground.

I mouthed the word *Stones?* to Little Ben. He nodded.

As she shut the van, Little Ben and I ducked behind a pile of potatoes and waited for her to pass us by.

But we weren't the only ones watching her. From all sides, orange-skinned men began to close in on her. *It's a good thing they don't know we're here,* I thought.

"HYACINTH!" roared Hungerford. He popped out of the mound of trash and bounded right to us. "I see that, that tattooed young woman!"

The Corkers and Minnie whirled around. Hungerford looked at them and then back at us. "Who, who are those orange gentlemen? Friends of yours?"

CHAPTER 29

A group of Corkers wobbled towards us, cutting us off from Minnie. "Can you clear a path?" I asked Hungerford. "We need to go—"

Before I could say "that way" and point, Hungerford roared out "Yes!" and bounded off in the wrong direction. He barreled into a Corker, sending him tumbling and creating a beautiful gap in the line of Corkers, precisely where we didn't need him to.

"Come back!" I yelled, but he didn't hear me over the noise of the crowd and just bounded enthusiastically out of sight.

On the opposite side of the market, I could see Minnie about to leave, unimpeded. So not only had Hungerford failed to help me, he had created a distraction that was letting her escape.

If I'd been a huge magical animal, I could have just bar-reled my way through to her, but unlike Hungerford and Oaroboarus, I didn't have the mass of several dozen people combined. Although . . . you know who did have the mass of several dozen people?

Several dozen people, that's who.

"Fire!" I yelled, and started pushing towards Minnie. "Fire!"

Little Ben caught on immediately. "Fire!" he yelled. "Flood! Famine! Sorry, I got carried away."

By that point, other people in the crowd had already picked up the call, setting off a stampede to the exit. If the Corkers had had the chance to squeeze together, they could have bounced the mob right off, but the mass of panicked market-goers surged over them too quickly. I saw several or-ange men bouncing over the crowd like balloons at a concert as we poured onto the street.

Minnie had a head start, but the weight of the suitcase must have slowed her down, and as we spilled out of the market, I spotted her across the street, heading into London Bridge Tube station.

We crossed as soon as the light changed, but by the time we got inside the station, she had a two-minute lead. "There!" Little Ben said, pointing down a flight of steps to a concourse below. We couldn't see her over the heads of the commuters, but we could see people stumbling over her suit-case, as though a wave of clumsiness were passing through the crowd.

"She's heading for the ticket gates. Do you have an Oyster?" I asked Little Ben as we ran down the steps.

"Yes!" He reached into his carpetbag and pulled out an oyster shell.

"No, not an actual oyster. An Oyster card. It's, like, a ticket for the Tube."

"I mostly travel by sewer."

"No problem." I reached into my pocket and pulled out two of the blue-and-white cards. "I don't trust Mom to carry hers. I'm sure she won't mind you using it."

We passed through the gates and spotted Minnie lugging her suitcase into an elevator. "This is our chance!" I said—but the doors closed just as we got there.

We turned around and ran back to the escalator.

In my short time in London, I had learned that it was a very diverse city. There were mosques and churches and synagogues and Hindu temples. But if there was one religious belief that all Londoners held with equal fervor, it was this:

Stand on the right. Walk on the left.

And the house of worship in which stand-on-the-righters met was the London Underground. If you weren't in a rush, you stood on the right-hand side of the escalator. That way, the left-hand side stayed free for anybody who had to get to a job interview, or meet a date, or beat a tattooed girl with a suitcase full of stolen magical stones to the ground floor.

And if you're feeling impatient because you want to know if we did beat the elevator, and all these words of explanation are getting in your way—well, then, you know exactly how

Little Ben and I felt when we got to the escalator and found a group of tourists standing on the right *and* left. Heretics!

"Excuse me," I said to the nearest sinner. She nodded and smiled at me, but she didn't move. If we had been on level ground, I would have just shoved my way through, but I couldn't risk sending someone toppling down the escalator. I turned to Little Ben. "Try every language you know," I told him. "Get them to move."

He cleared his throat. "*Excusez-moi? Enschuldigung? An-cay ee-way et-gay ast-pay? Con permiso? Me excusa?* 劳驾? *με συγχωρείτε?* عفواً. Um, I think that's it. Wait, was one of those Chinese? 哇!"

None of the languages worked, but by now, we were at the bottom of the escalator, and as the tourists piled off, we ran past them into a long white tunnel with yellow arches leading off on both sides.

"You go left, I'll go right," I said.

The platform through the right-hand arch was mobbed. If Minnie was there, I couldn't see her through all the people.

I could see a bench, though. I stood on it, giving me a view over everybody's head—and there she was, all the way at the other end, about to board a train.

There was no way I was going to make it over to her before the doors closed, so I clambered off the bench and dashed into the nearest carriage.

The doors closed, and we took off. As we rattled through the tunnel, I came up with a plan. At the next stop, I'd get off and push my way along the platform as far forwards as I could. If possible, I'd make it to her carriage. If not, I'd hop back on before the train left.

So when the train stopped, I got off as soon as the door opened. This station was much less crowded, which would have meant I could get all the way up to Minnie's carriage— if Minnie hadn't gotten off herself. As she stepped off, she glanced around and spotted me, and I noticed she wasn't holding the suitcase. Had she forgotten it, or had she handed it off to somebody else?

I didn't have long to contemplate the question, because she took off at a sprint. I ran after her, and as I did, I remembered another rule that's almost as sacred as "Stand on the right": no running on Underground platforms. *I'll be careful,* I thought. *I won't run into anybody.*

I ran into somebody.

Fortunately, instead of toppling into the gap between the train and the platform, he grabbed hold of something. Specifically, he grabbed hold of my arm, and just to be safe, I grabbed his.

"Sorry!" I said.

"Watch out—" he said, and then stared at me in amazement.

I stared back at him.

It was Dasra.

CHAPTER 30

"*You,*" we said simultaneously. Then we both said, "Let go of me."

I glanced down the platform. Minnie had already vanished. Without her heavy suitcase, she was probably already out of my reach. Better to hang on to the one bad guy I knew I had.

"I'll let go of you when you tell me what you're doing here," I said.

"I don't owe you anything, least of all an explanation."

"I don't need one. I know why you're here: you stopped me from following Minnie."

He arched an eyebrow at me. "If you don't need an explanation, then why don't you let me go? And by the way, *you* stopped *me* from following that girl."

"Carefully phrased," I said. "Were you following her to catch her . . . or to help her?"

He glared at me angrily. "I'm not going to dignify that with an answer."

"Then you aren't as good at going around the glasshouse as your grandma."

"Don't talk about my grandmother," he snarled, and with a sudden burst of strength, he yanked himself out of my grasp.

He hurried down the platform, and I hurried after him— although, I noticed, both of us were being careful not to run. We had learned our lesson.

"Give me one good reason not to call the police on you," I said.

"Be my guest, Miss Fugitive-from-a-high-security-magical-prison."

"That's so—you're so—RRRR!" I said. Apparently the ability to reduce me to speechlessness was a family trait.

"Now leave me alone," he said, "or *I'm* going to call the police on *you.*"

I stopped and let him vanish into the crowd. What else could I do?

I was accused of enchanted theft larceny. My mom and I had a bouncy but persistent magical army after us. I knew we were innocent, and I was pretty sure I knew who was guilty—but I had no way of proving it. And until I could, I was going to be a fugitive.

CHAPTER 31

"Maybe the reason you can't prove Dasra is her accomplice is, it's not true," Little Ben said.

I stared at him in disbelief. We were seated next to my mom, in front of Mr. Champney's desk of stacked stones, and we had just finished telling the historian everything that had happened.

"You think it's a coincidence that Lady Roslyn's grandson keeps popping up?" I asked.

"No, but there are lots of other explanations. Maybe he's trying to stop her, too."

"If he's not on her side, how does he always know where she's going to be?"

"How did *we* know where she was going to be? We looked at the evidence and made a deduction."

"Except for the time when we *followed Dasra right to her.*"

"Ahem." Mr. Champney cleared his throat. "Your friend is right, Hyacinth. You don't have enough evidence to know what the young man is up to. But you have more than enough evidence to know that you have thrust yourself into a dangerous situation. Whether this young woman is wielding magic fingers or a laser beam, she has something sharp enough to cut stone. And the government takes the threat seriously enough to send military forces after her." He focused his watery eyes on Mom. "Madam, when we spoke before, you refused to stop your daughter from embarking on this madness. Have you seen enough to change your mind?"

"I've seen my daughter face far worse," Mom said. "Um, I have, haven't I, honey?"

"You sure have," I told her.

Mr. Champney picked up a framed photograph from his desk and looked at it thoughtfully. "This is not a happy photo, but I keep it on my desk as a reminder. When you study history, it can seem bloodless. But it's made up of the joys and tragedies of real people." He turned it around to show it to us: a hospital bed with a child, an oxygen mask on her face. "I once had a wife and a child. There was a fire. My wife and daughter . . ." He stopped, his face contorted, as if he was trying to hold back tears. "They both survived . . . initially. But they had inhaled so much smoke . . ."

He couldn't go on. He lowered his head, tears finally streaming down his face. We all sat there in silence. Finally, he looked up at us with sudden intensity. "Mrs.

Herkanopoulos, if you had been through what I have been through, you would not take this so lightly."

"I am so, so sorry for your loss," Mom said. She put her hand on top of his. "If I could keep my daughter home safe with me for all eternity, I would. But I can't. There are secrets in my family that I don't understand, but I do know they almost killed her once. I would do anything to keep my daughter safe. *Anything*. In this case, that means letting her go out in the world and find out what those secrets are."

Mr. Champney sighed. "If you feel you must do this for your daughter's sake, then I cannot dissuade you. I, too, would do anything—" For a moment, his voice choked with tears again. Then he corrected himself. "*Would have done* anything for my family. Well. I have given you my warning. You must make your own choices and face your own consequences. All I can do is keep these children as far away from trouble as I am able. So, because you have been focused on the presence of this young man Dasra, you have failed to notice someone else who showed up repeatedly."

It was Little Ben who figured it out first. "Ooooh, Brigadier Beale!"

"Hold on," I said. "If you don't think Dasra is suspicious, you definitely can't think Brigadier Beale is. It's his job to chase Minnie Tickle. It would be suspicious if he *didn't* turn up."

"Precisely," Mr. Champney said. "The moments he wasn't there are the ones that seem most suspicious."

Little Ben nodded eagerly. "We never saw him at the

same time as the Precious Man," he said. "I mean, assuming it was the Precious Man driving the van."

I didn't buy it. "But *why* would he side with Minnie?"

"Remember what Inspector Sands said?" Little Ben asked. "Brigadier Beale was given 'full authority to quash magical disturbances. And as if on cue, a disturbance has arisen.'"

"You think he's faking these thefts to make it look like he's doing his job? That's a lot of work to get out of doing work."

"No, it's the other way around. The thefts are real. It's his investigation that's fake. And it's a brilliant plan!" Little Ben said, bouncing up and down on his chair in excitement. "If you were going to steal London's magical heritage, wouldn't you love to be the person who's supposed to protect it? You could always stay one step ahead of yourself."

"If he's the Precious Man, wouldn't that make Minnie Tickle his daughter? I don't think you'll find many dads who are willing to fire machine guns at their children."

Mr. Champney shook his head. "The Precious Man was Minnie Tickle's father in a legend recorded more than a century ago. I'm certain Beale isn't our young woman's actual father. That doesn't mean you can trust him."

"If it is him, although I still don't think it is, what are we supposed to do about it? Call the authorities? He *is* the authorities."

"If he is behind this, he must have been planning it for many years, as he steadily rose up through the ranks," Mr. Champney said. "You must be equally cautious. Find a safe place to hide. Stay there as long as you need to while figuring out your next move. Then you can return here, and we shall discuss it."

That wasn't what I wanted to hear, but I didn't know what else to say. We said our goodbyes and headed out.

As we stepped out onto Piccadilly, Mom started patting her pockets with a panicked look. "I've lost my Oyster card!"

I sighed. I had this conversation with her pretty much every day. "Mom, remember, I always hang on to it for you? Anyway, if you did lose it, it wouldn't be a big deal. We could—"

I stopped. Suddenly, I knew our next move. "To get past the safeguards that protected the underground rivers, Lady Roslyn had me use a magically charged umbrella," I told Little Ben. "And the way she charged it was by leaving it behind on the Tube. As she explained to me, the Baker Street Tube is the most dangerous magical nexus in London—and the Lost Property Office sits directly above it. That means that when an item passes through there, it gains an additional magical charge. And if you lose the item at another powerful spot on the Underground, you can double the effect."

"Ohhhh!" Little Ben said. "So Minnie Tickle didn't hand that suitcase full of stones to a confederate. She left it behind. She lost it on purpose!"

"That's my guess," I said. "But there's only one way to be sure."

CHAPTER 32

"I'm here to collect a suitcase full of ancient stones," I told the clerk behind the counter.

When I'd gone to the Lost Property Office of the London Underground with Lady Roslyn to collect a lost umbrella, it had clearly been a routine operation for them, and it had raised no eyebrows. This time, my request raised two. When the clerk finally lowered them, all he said was "Let me get my supervisor."

His supervisor also had raised eyebrows, although when they didn't go down, I realized it was a permanent condition: instead of running parallel to his eyes, his eyebrows ran at a forty-five-degree angle. It was kind of a striking effect, although it made his face hard to read.

"You're looking for missing stones?" he asked, staring at me with stunned surprise, or possibly complete neutrality.

"That's right," I said.

"And they belong to you?"

I hesitated. I had already demonstrated the explosive consequences of telling a lie around magic. Telling a lie in the most powerful magical nexus in London could be positively nuclear. On the other hand, surely people told lies near the Baker Street Tube all the time, and central London was still standing, so there must have been safeguards in place. I erred on the side of caution. "I'm very eager to have those stones returned," I glasshoused.

"Hmm," he said, looking skeptical, or possibly convinced. Then he shrugged and held out his hand. "I'm Roger Lock, by the way."

I shook Roger Lock's hand—and got a sudden electric shock, as if he were holding a joy buzzer. I jumped back. He turned his hand palm up to show me a tiny chip of stone, which looked as though it might have fallen off the Roman wall.

"The stones know," he said, with a look of satisfaction and/or disappointment. "I think we'll hold on to them for their rightful owner."

"That's good, right?" Little Ben said as we left. "If they won't give it to us, they won't give it to Minnie Tickle, either."

"But she must know that," I said. "She wouldn't have left them if she didn't have a plan for getting them back."

"How, though?" Little Ben asked.

As we stood there talking, a truck pulled into a nearby driveway, in front of a large metal grille. The driver climbed out and lifted up the grille, revealing the top of a large slide. He grabbed a large canvas sack from the truck and threw it down the slide. As it went down, I caught a glimpse of the label on the sack: LOST PROPERTY OFFICE.

"I wonder . . . ," I said. "Mom, distract that driver for me."

"How should I do that, sweetie? I'm not very good at distracting people. I believe people should be allowed to focus."

The driver was halfway done unloading, and we didn't have much time. Meanwhile, Mom bulldozed onwards. "There's nothing more annoying than when there's something important you need to do, and somebody keeps talking and talking and meanwhile your opportunity is slipping away and—"

"MOM! That's such a great point, I bet that man would love to hear all about it."

"Really?" Mom strode up to the driver. "Hello there, truck driver," she said. "My daughter thought you might like to learn about how frustrating it is when somebody interrupts what you're doing—"

He turned towards her, baffled and (more importantly) distracted. As Mom rattled on, I crept around the truck, took a running leap, and jumped for the slide—

—but before I landed on it, there was a loud *crack*, and I went flying backwards.

The driver spun around. "HEY!" he yelled. "What are you after?"

By way of answer, I ran. Mom and Little Ben followed

me. Apparently, the driver didn't want to leave his cargo, because he let us go.

Once we were out of his sight, we stopped and caught our breath.

"There must be some kind of filter on that slide," Little Ben said. "Nothing but actual lost property can get through."

I looked at Little Ben.

He looked at me.

"Are you thinking what I'm thinking?" I asked.

He grinned. "This is going to be sooooo cool."

CHAPTER 33

*T*hat evening, Mom got into a taxicab with a big suitcase. She had the taxi take her one block away. Then she got out, leaving the suitcase behind.

At least, I'm pretty sure that's what she did. Even though I was close to the action, I didn't exactly have the best view of it because I was inside the suitcase. Or, I should say, *we* were in the suitcase—Little Ben was crammed in there with me.

We had decided on a taxi instead of the Tube because we wouldn't have to wait too long before the cabdriver discovered us, and even with the air holes we had cut in the suitcase, we didn't want to spend any longer stuck in a suitcase than we had to.

Oh, and also, unattended luggage on the Tube sometimes gets blown up by the bomb squad.

"Miss! Miss! You forgot your— Oh, for heaven's sake.
She's disappeared already," the cabbie said.

"Lost Property Office, here we come," Little Ben whispered to me.

CHAPTER 34

I thought maybe the cabbie would hand us over to some body first, but he must have driven straight to the Lost Property Office, because after a few minutes of rumbling, the cab stopped and I heard the rattling of a metal grate being lifted. Then he opened the back door and yanked our suitcase out, and I could feel in my stomach that we were flying through the air. I had a moment of nerves: Were we going to run into that barrier again?

We didn't. The magical safeguards must have judged us sufficiently lost. We slid down at a sharp angle, and then we spun around, because it turns out that the baggage slide into the Lost Property Office goes in a spiral, which added dizziness to my list of complaints. Finally, we came to a sudden stop. Unfortunately, thanks to my old enemy Newton's laws, the suitcase came to a stop first, and then Little Ben's head stopped when it hit the nearest bit of suitcase, and then mine stopped when it hit Little Ben's head. But the important thing was, we had arrived.

We waited until we heard the truck start up and drive away, and a few minutes more for good measure.

"Think it's safe?" I whispered to Little Ben.

"As safe as it's going to get," he whispered back.

Using the string we had tied to the inside of the zipper, I unzipped the bag.

We toppled out, dizzy and achy. When we finished rubbing our foreheads and falling over, we clambered across the pile of suitcases and canvas bags that surrounded us and took in the scene.

We were in an industrial-looking room, with exposed air ducts on the low ceiling, and concrete bricks visible through the thin white paint of the wall. Long gray counters stretched from the blue spiral slide at our backs to the other end of the room, where tall rolling cages held hundreds of backpacks and suitcases.

The room was big enough for a dozen workers, but we had done well to get lost after business hours—there was nobody there but us.

"I bet these counters are for people to empty the bags out, to see if they can figure out who they belong to," Little Ben said.

"I guess not all bags come with chips of magically charged stones to identify the owners," I said.

We chose a metal cage and started pulling bags out. There were small backpacks with cartoon characters on them and massive ones suitable for camping. There were suitcases of all sizes, but none of them was the one we had seen Minnie Tickle lugging. None of them were even heavy enough to have stones inside.

"If this is the room where they do their first sorting, there must be another room for the next step," I told Little Ben.

We passed the sorting tables into a long hallway lined with shelves and more cages. We didn't find Minnie's suitcase, but when we went down a flight of stairs, we found a treasure trove.

It was another long corridor, once again lined with metal cages, but these were overflowing with umbrellas: small pocket umbrellas, giant golf umbrellas, somber black umbrellas, colorful children's umbrellas.

"Wow!" Little Ben said. "It's like something from the Arabian nights!"

"Sure, if the forty thieves were reeeeeally worried about their robes getting wet."

"Oooh, that one has a sword handle!" He tried to yank it out. "It must be jammed in."

"It's cool, but if it's not made of stone, it's not what we're looking for."

Ignoring me, Little Ben tried a bunch of other umbrellas in the same cage. They all slid out smoothly. Then he tried the sword-handled one. It didn't budge.

"It's an umbrella shaped like a sword, and I can't remove

it," he said. "Does that seem like it's part of the weird ten percent? It seems very ten-percenty to me."

I walked over, grasped the sword-shaped handle, and pulled the umbrella out easily. "See? You must have been pulling at a funny angle or someth—"

I stopped midword, interrupted by a sensation that was definitely not a typical umbrella-related one. It was like a brief electric shock shooting up my arm, followed by the feeling that the umbrella was almost a part of my hand. It was exactly what I had felt when I had picked up Bazalgette's Trowel, the very first magical item I ever encountered.

"I think this is a tosheroon," I told Little Ben. When Lady Roslyn and I had explored the sewers, we had encountered a group of toshers—scavengers of the enchanted items that washed up in London's magical underground rivers. Of all the things they searched for, the most valuable were called tosheroons—multiple magical items fused together into a new, more powerful one. This certainly looked like one, given that it started off like a sword and ended up like an umbrella. (Of course, I couldn't claim to completely understand the concept of tosheroons, given that the toshers somehow thought *I* was one. I never got a straight answer on why they thought that, or even how it was possible.)

I looked closely at the umbrella. It was encrusted with gleaming stones and as heavy as steel. In the middle of the handle, where the button would be on a normal umbrella, was a thick diamond. "I wonder . . . ," I said, and pushed the diamond. It clicked, and the umbrella whooshed open. I could now see that it wasn't an umbrella with a sword-shaped handle. It was both a sword and an umbrella at the same time—a sharp and shiny blade extended from the handle, gradually tapering until it became an ordinary umbrella shaft about halfway through.

"Cool!" Little Ben said.

"Except the umbrella part blocks me from using it as a sword."

"In modern-day London, an umbrella is probably more useful."

"Good point," I said, folding it closed. Since I didn't have a scabbard handy, I tucked it into my belt, and we moved deeper into the Lost Property Office.

We passed a room overflowing with scooters and baby carriages, then turned left into a chamber lined with long steel shelves. Each one was labeled with its contents, although the labels hardly did them justice. Sure, the CHILDREN'S TOYS shelf held children's toys, but I had never in my life seen such a jumble of stuffed animals, yo-yos, action figures, dolls, and windup helicopters. And then there was the LARGE MUSICAL INSTRUMENTS shelf, and the SMALL MUSICAL INSTRUMENTS shelf, and thousands of keys sealed in individual labeled envelopes, and, sitting in a corner all by itself, an urn labeled GRANDPA.

Past the last shelf, another slide led into darkness, through a hole in the floor.

"After you," Little Ben said.

I jumped in.

CHAPTER 35

$\mathcal{T}$he slide spiraled through the darkness and then it flattened out, and just as I was thinking *I wonder if I should brace myself,* I ran out of slide and smacked my bottom on the ground.

At least I had the presence of mind to roll out of the way before Little Ben came sliding down, so he didn't crash into me. "You don't have a flashlight in that bag of yours, do you?" I asked.

There was a rustling, and a click, and a narrow beam switched on.

A large sphinx leapt out of the darkness at us.

Little Ben and I screamed and jumped back, but the stone creature sat placidly on its massive haunches.

"I don't think it's actually moving," I said.

"N-no," Little Ben said. "It was a t-trick of the light. K-kind of an interesting effect, actually."

He cast his light around the room, revealing stone after stone—benches, crumbling walls, tiny fragments, starbursts and rectangles and statues and squares.

"I think we're in the right place," I said.

"I feel sorry for the workers who had to move all this stuff down here, without magic fingers."

I tapped the nearest statue. "Hello? Can you hear me?" It didn't budge.

"I think only the statues made from Coade stone are alive," Little Ben said. "These are regular stone. You can tell because they've been worn down by the elements—Coade stone lasts pretty much forever."

"I guess it's just us, then."

"I wouldn't say that," a voice said.

The lights switched on.

CHAPTER 36

$\mathscr{B}$y the door stood Roger Lock, the Lost Property Office employee who had buzzed me with the bit of Roman stone. I couldn't be sure, but his eyebrows seemed raised even more than usual.

"What are you doing here?" he demanded.

"We were . . . um . . ." My glasshousing powers failed me, so I told him the truth. "Everything in this room was stolen."

"Of course it was," he said.

Now it was my turn for raised eyebrows. "You knew that?"

"I read the newspapers. And I know Roman walls and medieval priories when I see them."

Little Ben couldn't believe what he was hearing, any more than I could. "And you're *leaving* it here?" he exclaimed.

"All lost items must remain at the Lost Property Office

for ninety days, waiting for their owners," Roger Lock said. "At the end of that period, if they haven't been claimed, we can dispose of them at our discretion. Usually that means donating them to a charity shop. In this case, we'll make sure everything goes back where it belongs."

"It's not that simple," I told him. "You used that stone chip on me, so I know you know magic is real, and—wait, you *did* know that, didn't you? I can't tell if you're surprised."

He laughed. "I work at the Lost Property Office. I see more enchanted items by nine AM than most people see in their lifetime."

"Then you must know that someone very powerful has gone through a lot of trouble to make sure all this stuff ended up right here. They wouldn't have done that if they didn't think they could get it back."

"There are elaborate safeguards in place," Roger Lock said. "No one can take something from here if it doesn't belong to them."

Little Ben piped up. "Then how can you get rid of things after ninety days?"

"That's when the law says a lost item stops belonging to its owner."

"So the law can change who owns something? And the magic will respect that?"

Lock nodded. "Law is a series of words that alters the nature of reality. It's a form of magic in and of itself."

"We've got a big problem," Little Ben said. "Minnie Tickle owns everything in here."

"What are you talking about?" I said. "We saw her steal stuff, right in front of us."

"Have you ever heard of the principle of market overt?" he asked.

"Market what?"

"It's an ancient law. If you buy something during daylight hours, in a market that has existed since time immemorial, it belongs to you—even if the person who sold it didn't own it in the first place."

I saw where he was going. "How long has Borough Market been around?"

"Nobody knows. A thousand years, at least, in that very spot. Parliament actually repealed the law of market overt decades ago—but the new law didn't say anything about magic items. I think they didn't want to publicly admit that magic exists. But that means magic items are still covered by the old law."

I turned to Roger Lock. "We saw Minnie Tickle give money to a merchant in Borough Market. We wondered why he didn't give her anything in exchange. I bet you she was buying the things she had already stolen."

"That's dismaying," Lock said. Maybe when your facial expressions were as unreadable as his, you got in the habit of explicitly stating your emotions. "But if she's truly the rightful owner of all this lost property, we'll have to give it to her as soon as she shows up to claim it."

I couldn't believe what I was hearing. "ARE YOU CRAZY????" I inquired politely.

"I won't enjoy doing it," Lock said. "I've spent my life making sure things go back to their owners. Handing sixty tons of London's heritage over to a thief will break my heart. But . . . Look, imagine it's World War Two, and you're a doctor with the Red Cross. You're allowed behind enemy lines to treat British POWs in an enemy camp. While you're there, you have the chance to shoot a couple of Nazi soldiers. Do you?"

"Of course not," I said.

"Why not?"

I had answered instinctively, but the more I thought about it, the more convinced I became. "Because shooting a few random Nazis won't end the war any sooner. All it would do is stop anybody from ever trusting the Red Cross again. There'd be thousands of deaths on my hands. Maybe more."

"Mr. Lock," Little Ben said, "I think it's great what you do. So many umbrellas! But you're not the Red Cross. If you break the rules, people just get wet. No offense!"

Lock didn't seem offended, although I'm not sure I'd know if he was. "The stakes are higher than you might think. Any item here might have been crucial to the destiny of its owner. That's why they built the Lost Property Office above a magical nexus: when an item passes through here, it returns to its owner with a magical charge, in case they need it to restore their life to its rightful path."

"But all these—" I gestured to the stones around us. "By your logic, every one of them is crucial, too. Millions of people passed them every day. Who knows how their absence will change those people's fates?"

"All the more reason to stick to the rules," Lock answered. "You're going to have to leave."

Little Ben headed for the door, but I wasn't giving up that easily. "No," I said.

"Excuse me?" Roger Lock said.

"This is the best lead we've got. We've been shot at and arrested and nearly drowned to get here, and we're not going to walk away."

Lock sighed. "I'm sorry to hear that. I've tried reason. Now, I'm afraid, I'm going to have to use force." He reached up over his shoulder, and for the first time, I noticed that he was wearing a scabbard on his back, crocheted out of red and green yarn. He reached into it and unsheathed his weapon.

It was a cricket bat.

"This was the second item ever left in the Lost Property Office," he said. "It's been down here for eight decades, gathering power."

He raised it. Bright light shot up its handle, coalescing at the tip and shaping itself into a ball of energy, hovering just above the bat.

He pulled the ball out of the air, then dropped it on the ground, letting it bounce.

As it came back up, he smashed it with the bat, sending it right at us.

CHAPTER 37

If I had had more experience being assaulted by magical glowing cricket balls, I might have had a rational plan in place. Instead, I acted instinctively and did something moderately crazy:

I pulled the umbrella out from my belt, opened it swiftly, and shielded myself and Little Ben.

The cricket ball smashed into the umbrella with enough force to send me staggering backwards—

—and then the ball exploded into a dozen flaming shards, which shattered into hundreds of flaming snowflakes, which hung in the air, twinkling, before fading away.

I lowered the umbrella.

Roger Lock was staring at me. He was speechless. His

jaw had dropped. His eyes had grown wide. His eyebrows had stayed exactly the same.

"Excalibrolly," he whispered, in an awestruck tone. "That umbrella was the very first item to end up here, decades ago. Nobody knew who turned it in—it just showed up, moments after our doors opened. The ninety days' period passed, and no one claimed it, so my predecessors tried to remove it, but it wouldn't budge. It became a rite of passage for all new employees to try to pull it out. A legend grew up that it could only be removed by one who was worthy to wield it. *Who are you?*"

"I guess I'm Excalibrolly's rightful owner," I said. "Does that mean we're on the same team?"

"I can't be on anybody's team. I took a vow of neutrality. But I do know somebody who might help: my husband Chapel is a Brother."

"What's a husband chapel?" Little Ben asked, at the same time I said, "You married your brother?"

"Not *my* brother," Lock said. "He's a Brother of the—"

He was interrupted by a loud explosion from somewhere above us. The lights flickered off and on.

The ancient segments of Roman wall, the giant stone sphinx, the tiny scattered pebbles, and all the rest began to vibrate. At first, I thought it was the aftershock of the explosion, but they kept on shaking. Then, like metal shavings moving towards a magnet, they slid towards the door.

"Minnie is here," I said.

"You must have been right about her buying them," Lock said. "They know their rightful owner."

"They know their *legal* owner," Little Ben said, shoving away a stone bench that pressed up against his leg like an overfriendly cat. "That's not the same thing."

"I can't make that distinction," Lock said.

Maybe I was just distracted by the stone elephant that was trying to run me over, but I could kind of see where Lock was coming from. Anyway, I was only going to convince him by arguing on his terms. So I said, "I understand. You have to play by Red Cross rules. But Excalibrolly has chosen me as its owner, and Minnie takes things away from their owners, and it's your sworn duty to help people keep things they own. So don't you have to help me, at least a little?"

He pointed to a stone sarcophagus, quivering eagerly in the far corner. "Let's get the lid off that. You can hide in there while . . ." He gritted his teeth and looked almost dismayed. "While I help this thief collect her ill-gotten gains. Good luck."

CHAPTER 38

The good thing about hiding in a stone sarcophagus is, you're in a lightproof, soundproof container, and when the lid slams down, nobody can see you.

The bad thing about hiding in a stone sarcophagus is, you're in a lightproof, soundproof container, and when the lid slams down, you have no idea what's going on outside it.

The *worst* thing about hiding in a stone sarcophagus is, it's a sarcophagus. As in, a big box for what's left of a dead person.

"Did you happen to read the name on the outside of this thing?" I asked Little Ben as I tried to arrange the bones so that I wasn't actually lying on top of them.

"I wish I had," Little Ben said. "It seems rude to be this close to someone without being introduced."

The sarcophagus tilted, sending us and the bones sliding around. Then it straightened out, and a few minutes later, the faint rumble of an engine came through the thick stone.

"The Precious Man's van?" Little Ben asked.

"That would be my guess," I said.

Little Ben and the dead guy and I rumbled along for a good twenty or thirty minutes. At one point, I tried to call Mom, just to check in with her, but I didn't have any reception—the sarcophagus hadn't been built with the mobile phone needs of its inhabitants in mind.

Then the rumbling stopped, and Little Ben and Anonymous Bones and I got to enjoy a bonus few minutes of being tilted into each other, presumably as Minnie Tickle levitated us somewhere.

Finally, we thumped back down onto the ground. We waited a few more minutes, and then I pushed up on the lid of the sarcophagus.

It didn't budge. Add "Easy to open from the inside" to that list of things that the sarcophagus industry really needs to pay more attention to.

Little Ben and I shoved and grunted, and a little crack of light appeared along the edge. We pushed until the crack grew big enough for us to peer out of. There was no sign of Minnie Tickle or anybody else, so we went back to pushing and grunting until finally the crack was big enough to squeeze through.

We were in a tall chamber, shaped like a shoe box standing on its narrowest side. It seemed to be built out of gray bricks, although a thick coating of dirt and grease made it hard to see their original color.

The height of the room and its obvious age gave it a certain dim beauty, even though it was almost entirely unadorned. There was a single decoration on each wall: a giant wheel, painted in fading white. Something about it looked familiar, but I couldn't quite place it.

To our left, there was a series of wide but shallow steps running three quarters of the way up to the ceiling. "Those steps don't go anywhere," I pointed out.

"Are they steps?" Little Ben said. "They look more like the seats in an amphitheater to me."

"An amphitheater for elves, maybe," I said. "You'd have to have an awfully tiny butt to sit in them."

If it was an amphitheater, we were standing in the part where the show would take place, a narrow rectangle of brick floor, crowded with the stone objects we had last seen in the Lost Property Office.

"This place must be important," Little Ben said. "Why else would Minnie work so hard to get this stuff here?"

"But then why would she leave? And how did she get out?" If there was an exit, it must have been hidden behind the mass of statues and plinths and architectural bric-a-brac.

"Maybe there's a clue in one of these things," Little Ben said. We looked under and behind and inside everything we could. Behind one gigantic stone urn, we thought we saw the edge of a door, but no matter how much we pushed, the urn wouldn't budge.

"Maybe there's something inside the urn that's making it even heavier. Help me up," I told Little Ben. He crouched down, and I clambered up on his shoulders, then pulled myself up on what looked like a medieval arch, until I could look down into the urn.

"Oh, for heaven's sake!" I exclaimed.

"What is it? Is it something cool?" Little Ben asked.

From inside the urn, Dasra looked up at me. "Are you going to stand there gawking, or are you going to get me out of here?"

CHAPTER 39

"*I* don't know," I said. "It seems to me that inside an urn isn't a bad place to keep Lady Roslyn's grandson, if you've got him there."

"Really?" Dasra said. "I thought you were the one who didn't believe in judging people by their ancestors."

That stung a little, but I wasn't going to show it. "I judge people by their actions," I said. "And so far, yours haven't given me any reason to trust you."

"*I* haven't given you any reason to trust *me*? You're the one who framed my grandmother."

"What are you talking about? She tried to kill my mom."

He shook his head. "That can't be true."

"I saw it with my own eyes."

He flinched and held his breath. Was he waiting to see if

things started exploding and collapsing? That would mean he thought I was lying. Which would mean he really thought Lady Roslyn was innocent. "Think about what your grand-mother told you," I said. "How did she phrase it?"

Dasra looked even more indignant than before. "Are you suggesting she glasshoused me? She would *never*—" And then he stopped.

"I know that look," I said. "That's the look I get when-ever I think back on something Lady Roslyn said and realize it was deliberately misleading but technically true."

When he spoke again, it was in a near whisper. "She told me she needed your mother's blood to take control of the riv-ers, but she said she was just using a few drops when you showed up. She never said what she did *after* you showed up. And she said, 'That young lady told the police I tried to kill her mother, and the fools believed it.' She never said it was a lie. In fact, you would have been surrounded by magic when you said it—you couldn't have lied. Why didn't I see that?"

He looked like he was about to cry. I felt something I would never have thought I could feel for Lady Roslyn's grandson: sympathy. I held out my hand. "Let's get you out of this urn," I said.

The good feelings lasted until we had climbed down to the ground. Dasra turned to me and said, "She was wrong to use violence. That doesn't mean her basic point was wrong. Some people are better qualified to be in charge."

"People like you and your grandmother, I'm guessing?" I said.

"Yes," Dasra said. "And people like you."

Okay, that was not the answer I expected. "I'm nothing like Lady Roslyn."

"Really? Before you stopped my grandmother—before you took actions that could shape the future of London—did you put it to a citywide vote?"

"No, but not because I thought I was better than anybody else. We were the only ones who were there to stop her."

"Exactly," Dasra said. "And why were you there?"

I saw where he was going with this. "It was because *she* thought my family history was important, not me."

"But she was right, wasn't she? Objectively speaking, you saw how powerful your mother's blood was. Your family history gave you the opportunity to influence events, and you seized that opportunity."

"Guys—" Little Ben said, but I wasn't going to be distracted.

"What do you know about my family history? What did Lady Roslyn tell you?"

"She said that for centuries the Herkanopoulos family had been caretakers of the magical power that runs beneath London. She said that generation after generation of Herkanopouloses had provided one child to serve each river, but your aunts had abandoned their duties. That's why she had to step in."

There were no explosions, and in any case, I didn't need a magical lie detector to believe what Dasra was telling me. It all fit. The women in the painting on the wall of the Mail

Rail and in the statues in the sacred place of the Fleet—they must have been my ancestors, which was why they looked so much like my mom and my aunts. And the sacred places of the rivers would have been important to my grandmother and my aunts, which was why they came to one of them when they were deciding whether to leave London.

But if Dasra's information answered some questions, it raised more. "What else did your grandmother tell—"

"GUYS!" said Little Ben. "I think I've figured out where we are. Stop and listen for a moment. It's urgent."

The three of us fell quiet. We could hear faint traffic noises, interrupted occasionally by an echoed *clang*. And in the distance, a faint cawing.

"Sea gulls?" I asked.

"That's right," Little Ben said. "We're above water, but we're under cars, and we're surrounded by metal. We're inside a bridge. I think this is one of the bascule chambers of Tower Bridge."

"I was with you up until *bascule*," I told him.

"It's French for something that rocks back and forth," Dasra said. "*Jeu de bascule* is a seesaw. *Cheval à bascule* is a rocking horse."

"Thanks, that's really helpful," I said. "So this is where they keep the seesaws?"

"Kind of," Little Ben said. "Tower Bridge is what's called a bascule bridge. It's like two giant seesaws facing each other. When they raise the bridge, both seesaws go up at once."

"So what's this room for?"

Little Ben made seesaws out of his hands and tilted them while he spoke, to show me what he meant. "When one half of a seesaw goes up, the other half has to go down. So when the road part of Tower Bridge goes up, the other part goes down, into this room. There's one of these chambers on each side of the bridge. Not many people get to see them!"

"We're very lucky," I agreed. "Now, if that's all you wanted to say—"

"One more thing. The part that goes down into this room? It's huge. It has to be as heavy as half of Tower Bridge in order to lift it up." He pointed to the ceiling. "And that's the bottom of it. And when the bridge goes up, that giant weight comes swinging down into this room. And anything in the room, whether it's made out of stone or skin and bones, is going to get crushed."

"We'd better get out of here," I said.

"FAST," Dasra added, and I was about to tell him not to order me around when I followed his gaze up to the ceiling.

It was coming down.

"They're raising the bridge," whispered Little Ben.

CHAPTER 40

It's amazing how fast you can move when you're in danger of getting squashed. I ran back to the urn where I had found Dasra and clambered to the top like I had rocket shoes. My butt planted on top of the urn, I wedged my feet against the wall. "We've got to move this away from the door," I called down. "You guys push from below!"

Even with the three of us pushing—even with my leverage—it wouldn't budge.

The ceiling lowered steadily, swinging downwards over the shallow brick steps.

"Come *on*," Dasra said. I didn't know whether he was talking to himself, or the others, or the urn.

"On the count of three," I said. "Give it everything you've got. One . . . two . . . three!"

With a last bit of energy, we sent the urn toppling. I fell down to the floor, right in front of a newly accessible stone door. Relieved, I grabbed the handle and pulled—but instead of swinging open, the door toppled towards me.

I dove out of the way.

Where the door had stood, there was nothing but brick. The door had been just another stolen architectural detail, leaned up against a solid wall.

"There!" Little Ben said. When the urn had fallen over, it had nudged a giant stone head, giving us a glimpse of an actual real doorway, with genuine hallway on the other side.

The only problem was, the ceiling had nearly reached it.

"Forward march!" I said, climbing over a table-sized stone sundial. I got to the giant stone head as the ceiling swung into it from the other side, toppling it straight towards me.

"Sideways scramble!" I said, leaping to the side as the head smashed into the spot where I had been.

For an instant, I had a clear path. With the giant head out of my way, I could jump straight out into the hallway outside. The problem was, I was the only one close enough to make it through before the ceiling blocked the way entirely. I'd be leaving Little Ben and Dasra behind.

I only had a fraction of a second to decide—but I didn't need that long. There was no way I was going to leave Little Ben to be squashed. (And if I happened to save Dasra in the process—well, he probably deserved to live, too.)

So I jumped back towards the far wall, grabbing at Little

Ben's arm to pull him along. "Stop!" he yelled. "My foot is stuck in a philtrum!" I looked down. When the giant head had toppled, the bit between its giant nose and its giant upper lip had landed on Little Ben's ankle, trapping it there.

Dasra knelt down, bracing his shoulder under one giant eye, and I did the same with the other. We both strained upwards, and the head lifted a bit, freeing Little Ben.

We scrambled madly away from the oncoming ceiling. As it moved forwards, it swept up the statues and walls and oddly shaped stones, sending them tumbling and smashing into each other. It was like trying to run over balls in a bingo cage.

Dasra stumbled and flew forwards. As he threw out his hands to catch himself, one arm plunged between two halves of a fractured Roman wall. I grabbed him by the armpits and yanked him up.

And then we were safely at the far wall, which was a relief, until I turned around and saw the wave of churning stone being swept towards me in slow motion.

"When the bridge opens, does it stick straight up?" I asked Little Ben.

"Almost, but not quite."

The wave of stone was half as high as the chamber, and ten feet away.

"So that means the other end doesn't go all the way down?" Dasra asked. "If we press up against this wall—"

"—instead of getting smashed by the ceiling, we'll get smashed by all the stone," Little Ben answered.

The wave of stone was three quarters as high as the

chamber, and five feet away. Little mini-waves of rubble broke away from it, lapping at our feet.

"Look!" In the corner, about two feet from the wall, two pieces of iron stuck up from the floor. "The ceiling must rest against those. If we can shelter behind something . . . Help me lift this!" I grabbed one edge of a large stone slab.

The wave was nearly to the ceiling, and two feet away.

Dasra and Little Ben grabbed the other sides of the block, and with a burst of speed I would not have thought our tired muscles were capable of, we leaned it against the wall, with its bottom propped against those two iron pieces on the floor.

"Get in!" I yelled, and we dove under our improvised lean-to as the wave of stone crested and crashed, sending statues and finials and cornices and pedestals and a heavy rain of unidentifiable smashed bits pounding down where we had been standing.

For what seemed like ages, the world was nothing but thunder in my ears, and white dust in my lungs, and our shelter shaking like it was going to collapse—

—but it held.

The thunder stopped, and all we could hear was occasional crackling and thumping as the stones shifted. Everything was pitch black.

"Little Ben, do you still have that flashlight?"

"No, my carpetbag is somewhere out there. I'm guessing it's ground to bits."

I fished my phone out of my pocket and flipped it open, using the faint light of the screen to look around. If Mom had gotten me a smartphone, like I was always asking, it would have had a built-in flashlight, but I had to make do with what I had.

Through the dimness and the slowly thinning cloud of dust, I could see a solid wall of shattered fragments blocking the way.

We were trapped.

CHAPTER 41

While I had my phone out, I glanced at the screen: zero bars, which was what I had expected, with a room full of stone and an entire bridge standing in the way of the signal.

"Looks like we're stuck here for a while," I said.

"Let's pass the time telling stories!" Little Ben said.

"Good idea. Dasra, you can start by telling me what else you know about my family."

"I've told you everything I know about them."

"Then tell me about *your* family. Are you on some kind of mission from your grandmother? Why do you keep showing up when something bad is about to happen?"

I didn't mean to antagonize him. I thought it was a fair question. Dasra didn't. "I don't owe you any explanations," he said. "I don't owe you *anything.*"

"I saved your life. Your arm was stuck."

"And I saved yours about four seconds later. Remember? It took all three of us to lean the slab against the wall."

"Then you only saved one third of my life. I saved all of yours. You owe me two thirds of a life's worth of explanation."

"I saw your face when I told you about your family. You were stunned. It was major news to you."

"It was one-third-of-a-life stunned, at most. You still owe me a third."

He crossed his arms and looked stubbornly away.

An awkward silence followed, broken only by the occasional *chank* of stone fragments settling. Then the *chanks* turned into a roar. "The bridge must be going back down," Little Ben yelled over the cacophony.

The rubble slid away, and I poked my head out. Little Ben was right—the ceiling was slowly rotating back into place, letting the wave of stones slide backwards, like a tide made out of pebbles.

And pebbles were all that was left. All of the treasures that had existed minutes ago—the statues, the crypts, the walls, even the fragmented but still recognizable segments of larger items—had been reduced to smashed bits. Every item Minnie had stolen represented years of study and hundreds of hours of work by masons and sculptors, followed by centuries of effort to protect and preserve them. And they had been destroyed in seconds. I could almost hear the stones' creators crying.

Wait—forget the "almost." I *could* hear them. As the

stone wave flowed out, the clashing of pebbles began to sound like moaning, and then like sighing and weeping, and in moments, the noises of despair were deafening.

I clapped my hands to my ears.

As the weeping continued, the stone tide flowed out farther, and as it lowered, it revealed the weepers. The chamber was full of ghosts, their clothes as varied as the centuries they came from, all holding hammers and chisels that didn't change much across the years.

I had seen ghosts before, and been terrified, but these ones weren't frightening. They were heartbreaking. I lowered my hands; shutting out their cries seemed like an insult to them. And I began to weep with them.

By their spectral flicker, and by the glow of the room lights that were no longer blocked, I could see Dasra and Little Ben. Neither of them seemed put off by a roomful of ghostly crying craftspeople.

"Are you okay?" Little Ben asked, putting a friendly hand on my arm.

I stared at him in disbelief. "Can't you see them?"

"All the smashed things? Of course. It's really sad."

"No, the ghosts."

Now it was his and Dasra's turn to stare at me. "This is no time for joking—" Dasra started, but stopped when he saw my expression. "You really see ghosts?"

I didn't answer, because the uncoordinated weeping had turned into a single, unified moan. The ghosts stretched their arms up in the air, holding their tools high, and began to lift off the ground. They merged as they rose, until the air was filled with a glowing cloud. It swooped towards the wall, as if it was about to pass through it, but then the circle painted on the wall erupted in flame, and the cloud bounced off it.

Dasra and Little Ben gasped. They must have seen the flames, even if they couldn't see the ghosts.

The cloud swooped to the other side, but the circle there, too, erupted, and the cloud bounced off again.

The moaning grew louder. Back and forth the cloud flew, faster and faster. The circles of flame stretched out farther and farther, becoming cylinders, until finally they met in the middle of the room, surrounding the cloud. There was an eruption of light and noise—

— and the cylinder of flame split again, each half arcing down until it met the surface of the crushed stone mass. For a moment, the stones shook with energy, and the moaning was deafening, and then—

—silence. The cloud was gone. The flames were gone.

Something shiny and metal hung in the air, in the dead center of the room. It floated for a moment, and then dropped downwards at an angle, flying straight into my hand.

It was a small chisel. It looked like one of the tools the ghosts had wielded, but it was solid and real, as if the flames had forged it into something physical.

I slipped it into my pocket. The ghosts were gone, and their work was destroyed—but I was not going to forget them.

CHAPTER 42

"What just happened?" Little Ben asked. "Where did that chisel come from?"

"I don't understand why you couldn't see them," I said. "The room was full of—"

"Shh!" Dasra said.

When the tide of stone had settled, it had revealed two doorways on either side of the room. There were footsteps coming from the one on the right.

I crawled back under the slab, with Little Ben and Dasra close behind.

We had just made it under the slab when it floated up above our heads. So did all the smashed rubble.

Minnie was here.

As long as we were under the veil of crushed stone, we

were blocked from her view. We could crawl under it without her seeing us. But which way should we go? The rational choice was the empty left-hand corridor. She'd never know we were there, and we could wait until she headed out and then follow her, and we could get some sort of proof that she was guilty and we were innocent. After staying out of her sight all this time, there was absolutely no reason to go right.

But I wanted to avenge the ghosts of all those artists and craftspeople. I wanted to make her pay for her crimes against creativity.

I should go left, I thought.

I went right.

When you've got a rough, damp brick floor beneath you, and a ceiling of crushed stone hovering above you, it's not pleasant to crawl quickly, but I was fueled by anger. I zoomed, ignoring the scraping I was giving my knees and the repeated bumps I was giving my head.

"Wrong way," Little Ben whispered. I ignored him, too.

Now that I was nearly at the door, I could see Minnie's legs beneath the hovering stone. I slammed my shoulder into them, and she went toppling backwards.

Like I said, I was too clogged up with anger and grief to think clearly. So not only did I ignore a bunch of reasons I shouldn't knock Minnie over, I didn't even think of the biggest one. The rocks were levitating because she had her finger pointed at them, which meant that when she flew backwards, her finger made a wild arc, and the previously orderly bunch of floating rocks flew up in the air.

And as she fell completely backwards, her finger pointed completely away from the rocks, breaking the magical connection and letting them plummet back to the floor . . .

. . . where Dasra and Little Ben were still crawling.

They jumped to their feet and sprinted for the doorway, making it out as several tons of crushed London architecture smashed behind them—

—and several pounds of it fell on my head.

The hallway spun and filled up with clouds. I closed my eyes, leaned against the white brick wall, and took a deep breath. When I opened my eyes again, the room wasn't spinning and the stars were gone.

But the clouds were still there. No, not clouds: masses of stone, pouring out of the bascule chamber as Minnie hurried them along with urgent gestures.

Oh, and they were coming straight at me.

I ducked.

Her left hand busy levitating stuff, Minnie pointed her right hand at the floor, and jets erupted from her fingers. She floated up, the river of mineral debris parting around her. Riding it like a magic carpet, she shot away.

We chased her into a round brick chamber, ten stories high, with a metal staircase spiraling along the wall. After all the running I had done since I arrived in London, I was in pretty good shape, and even using magic, dragging along a couple of tons of stone seemed to slow Minnie down. Although she flew straight up through the center of the room and we had to run up the staircase, getting dizzier and more breathless as we went, we weren't *too* far behind her when we got to the top.

Which meant we weren't too far behind her as we chased her into what must have been the control room for the bridge—a narrow chamber filled with huge levers and polished brass dials. The dawn sun streamed through the windows, and I wondered briefly how long it had been since I got out of bed the previous morning, but I didn't think about it for long. I had a more urgent concern:

Minnie was riding a smashed stone elevator down to the river. As the rubble reached the water, it reassembled itself into a barge fit for Cleopatra.

CHAPTER 43

$\mathcal{I}$ gave a moment's thought to jumping after her, but I knew immediately that would be madness. If I landed on the boat, I'd break my spine. And if I landed in the water—well, I had seen somebody fall into the Thames once, and she had very nearly drowned. I wasn't going to take that risk.

So as the boat took off upstream, my only option was to run along the bank of the river after it. I'd never keep up with it, but I had to try. I turned around and was nearly run over by a bus.

Wait—not a bus. A giant pig in a bus costume, with a replacement carpetbag in his mouth.

"Oaroboarus!"

AT YOUR
SERVICE

"Climb aboard," Mom said. She was sitting on Oaroboarus's back.

"Mom? How'd you find me?"

Hungerford bounded up. "I, I, I'm delighted to take the credit for this happy reunion. The city's Coade stone guardians told me where to find this, this stunning specimen of the porcine breed, and they also tracked the van in, in, in which you so bravely traveled."

Little Ben climbed up onto Oaroboarus. Oaroboarus looked back and forth between me and Dasra.

A day ago, I would have gladly left Dasra behind. But with the whole saving-each-other's-life thing, I was starting to warm up to him a little.

Not enough to let him go unsupervised, though. "You ride Oaroboarus with my mom and Little Ben," I told him. "I'll take Hungerford."

"With pleasure, I, I, I shall—"

I wouldn't have thought a statue could blush, but Hungerford turned the color of red marble. "That's, that's, that's . . . Well, I suppose that's probably merited." He held his mouth up to Oaroboarus's nose and exhaled.

"Oaroboarus! She's getting away!" I said.

I knew that arguing with him was only going to waste more time. Fortunately, Hungerford seemed willing to do whatever Oaroboarus asked. The lion was cowed by the pig.

He walked forwards a few steps in his usual stumbling, over-eager gait, but he managed to walk straight.

Oaroboarus nodded, although he still looked skeptical.

Hungerford knelt. I grabbed his mane and pulled myself up as Dasra climbed on Oaroboarus.

If Oaroboarus had asked me what our next move should be, I wouldn't have said, "Jump over the side of the bridge," but he didn't ask. He just jumped. Little Ben whooped with excitement as they vanished over the side, and a moment later, Hungerford followed. We plummeted a good twenty feet down onto a walkway that ran along the river, Hungerford's feet smashing the pavement beneath him into fragments.

In the time it had taken to get us moving, Minnie had progressed farther along the river, but she hadn't gotten as far as I would have expected. She was gliding along at a leisurely pace, waving at the early-morning joggers along the path.

We were attracting plenty of attention ourselves. Hungerford hadn't bothered with a disguise, and Oaroboarus was getting a lot more staring and pointing than he had before. Maybe it was harder for people to convince themselves that he was a real bus when he was accompanied by a massive stone lion and a tattooed girl on a rubble barge.

"How come you don't have to wear a disguise like Oaroboarus?" I asked Hungerford.

"We Coade stones are part of the, the very architectural fabric of the city, and as such, the authorities trust us to, to pass entirely unnoticed," he roared as he smashed into a coffee stand and sent it crashing into the river, while the barista ran screaming away.

Up ahead, Minnie's barge came to rest in front of London Bridge. Oaroboarus locked his legs and glided to a perfectly smooth stop. Hungerford tried to imitate him, toppled over, and sent me flying.

While the others climbed down from Oaroboarus, I scrambled to my feet. Meanwhile, on the river, Minnie lifted her hands, and her barge disassembled itself, long streams of rubble arcing into the river, until only half of it was left above the surface.

"Ooh, I know what she's doing," Little Ben said. "That's how they made bridges in olden times. They started by dumping a bunch of stone debris into the river to make a base."

"She's making a bridge?"

"Not just any bridge. She's laying the foundations exactly where Old London Bridge was."

Even if I'd known what to say to that, Little Ben wouldn't have been able to hear me, thanks to the sound of the helicopter that rose up from behind a nearby building. On London Bridge (the one that was already there, that is), Brigadier Beale leapt to his feet from a camouflaged hunting blind, and a bunch of Corkers popped up, slingshot guns in hand.

If I had trusted Beale, I would have been glad of the reinforcements. As it was, I mostly just didn't want him to notice me. I sank out of sight behind the low wall that stood between the path and the river. Little Ben did, too, and even Mom took the hint and crouched down.

Hungerford, meanwhile, stood there in full view, talking in his usual roar. "Who is, is, is that visibly stouthearted military man? Do you suppose he, he—"

Oaroboarus shoved Hungerford with his snout. "Careful there, old friend, you, you might not have realized—" Another shove. "Oops! We, we seem to be moving at cross-purposes—"

Oaroboarus pushed Hungerford harder, bulldozing him towards a path that led away from the river, between two buildings. As the two of them vanished, I could hear Hungerford's voice growing fainter. "Why are we, we quitting the field of battle? I would love a, a, a private conference, but this is neither the time nor—"

Fortunately, two more helicopters swung into view, and the noise of their rotors drowned out Hungerford's protests.

Beale's intense eyes stayed focused on Minnie, who had been hovering in place above the river, as if waiting for him to make the next move.

He made it.

He lifted a walkie-talkie and barked a single word into it. I couldn't hear it over the helicopters, but based on the fact that every Corker raised his weapon, I was pretty sure that the word was "Ready."

Seemingly unfazed, Minnie raised both hands high in the air. Was she surrendering? But as her tattoos swirled more urgently than ever before, the remains of her barge shot upwards, splitting into multiple columns.

Beale barked another word. The Corkers aimed their

slingshot guns. Similar weapons on the helicopters whirred to life, ready to bombard Minnie with—

Oh, no, I thought. Suddenly, I knew why Minnie's progress up the river had been so slow and so dramatic. She wanted to be seen. She wanted Beale to show up. *She wanted him to fire at her.*

I leapt to my feet. "Stop!" I called. "Whatever you do, don't—"

Beale didn't even notice me. He yelled another command, and the air exploded with projectiles. Pebbles from the machine guns smashed into Minnie's debris, but they simply bounced off and froze into high arches joining the columns. It was like watching a super-fast, super-heavy connect-the-dots, and within seconds, the entire picture took shape: nineteen stone arches, spanning the river from bank to bank. A new bridge, hovering in the air above the Thames.

The firing stopped. Whether it was because Beale finally realized he was playing into Minnie's hands or just because they ran out of ammo, I didn't know.

Hungerford chose that moment to burst back from the path, dragging Oaroboarus, who had the lion's stone tail clenched in his mouth in a futile effort to pull him away. "Don't shoo me away at this, this, this critical juncture! That pig has no, no, no sense of appropriate timing!" Hungerford roared, his voice booming out across the newly silent river.

That got Brigadier Beale's attention. His face, already tight with anger, grew almost purple. "GET THEM!" he yelled.

A dozen Corkers bounded towards us.

CHAPTER 44

With a dramatic flourish, Minnie let her creation drop.

As the arches plunged into the Thames, the newly made bridge somehow stayed perfectly intact. The buildings already on the riverbank were not so lucky. Across the river from us, the bridge crashed into a building near an old church, splitting it in half. And the near end of the bridge crashed into the base of a modern office tower above our heads. We dove out of the way as shards of glass and chunks of concrete smashed against the ground where we had been standing.

When I finished screaming and leaping, I was actually kind of relieved, because the new bridge now stood between us and the Corkers.

My relief didn't last long. With a *sproing*, a bouncing Corker came flying up from the other side. But as soon as he was above Minnie's new bridge, the *sproing* was replaced by a *bzzt,* and he crashed into some invisible magical shield, like a bug flying into an electrified fence.

That bought us some time, but I was sure they'd figure out a way over the bridge soon.

"Oaroboarus!" I said. He knelt down, and Mom, Little Ben, and I climbed up.

"You can go with Hungerford," I told Dasra. This was totally because he was now in as much trouble with Brigadier Beale as we were, and therefore I knew he'd stick with us, and not at all because, if Hungerford happened to knock him off, Dasra might benefit from a little undignified falling to the ground. (Okay, maybe it was a *little* because of the falling-to-the-ground thing.)

We took off down the side passage. As we did, I heard a series of splashes from behind us. I glanced over my shoulder to see Corkers popping out of the river and onto the shore. Even if they couldn't go over the bridge, it seemed, they could go under it.

As we ran out of the passage, we nearly crashed into a tall man who was running into it. With astonishing agility, he somersaulted out of the way, drew a sword from a back scabbard in midair, and landed, brandishing it dramatically.

"I bid you welcome to—oh, bother." Before he could finish his proclamation, the scabbard tumbled off his back and collapsed at his feet, a mass of bright yarn.

And just like that, as he bent down to collect it, I knew who he was. "You're Roger Lock's husband," I said.

"How'd you—"

"No time. My name's Hyacinth. He said you'd help us. We've got to hide."

His expression switched to intense focus. "Right. Follow me." He spun on his heels, led us down a nearby staircase, and pushed open a dinged-up door. "Through here." The humans ran in. Although Oaroboarus was wider than Hungerford, the giant pig made it inside without damaging the door, while Hungerford cracked the wood on the doorway as he squeezed through.

The man followed us in and shut the door behind him. "You'll be safe here," he said. "But how did you know who I was?"

"Roger had a scabbard exactly like yours."

I don't know if opposites always attract, but it was certainly true in this case. Unlike Roger Lock, this man had the most expressive face I had ever seen. It showed equal parts annoyance and affection at the mention of the scabbard. But when he spoke, it was in a clipped, neutral tone, as though his voice didn't know that his face was giving everything away.

"Scabbard was gift of Roger's mum. Matching set. Not entirely practical." He extended his hand. "Chapel's the name. Roger told me about you. As much as he could. His oath and all. Knew you'd turn up at headquarters sooner or later."

We looked around at the dingy room, decorated with a few ancient tapestries that were mostly hidden behind a stack of stained cardboard boxes. An old TV sat in a back corner, muted but tuned to a news report. The overall effect was not particularly impressive. "Headquarters?"

"Oh, yes. Never finished my greeting." Chapel straightened, and his face glowed with pride. He spoke what was, for him, a remarkably long speech. "I bid you welcome to the ancient headquarters of the Brethren of the Bridge, protectors of London's bridges." Then the pride sank away and he looked embarrassed. "HQ used to be the whole city block," he said neutrally. "Only basement now."

"Lady Roslyn once told me that when the secret rivers reach the Thames, they all get mixed together, and their powers are diluted," I said.

"True. But not the whole story."

"That seems to be kind of a theme with Lady Roslyn," I said.

"Millennia ago, Peter de Colechurch figured it out. A priest. Founded the Brethren. Built a bridge with tons of arches—enough to separate out the power of each river."

"So if Little Ben is right and Minnie has rebuilt old London Bridge . . . will it give her control of all the rivers that flow into it?"

"Possibly," Chapel said. He pointed to the stained cardboard boxes. "Answer might be in there. All the Brethren's records."

"Oooh, files!" Little Ben said. "Can I look through them?"

"Wish you would. Always meant to, but can't get through 'em. More of a fighter than a reader. Brethren used to have big team of monks for brainy stuff. Just me, now."

"But why?" I asked as Little Ben eagerly opened up a

box. "If London Bridge is so powerful, shouldn't there be an army to protect it?"

Nostalgia and regret chased each other across Chapel's face. "Bridge *was* powerful. Too powerful. Factions always fighting over it. Egalitarians about to gain control, so Inheritors tore down old bridge. Built new one with fewer arches. No magical powers. Brethren shrank. Then: 1960s. Rogue Egalitarian. Managed to activate bridge magically, somehow. Plot foiled. Entire bridge dismantled. Sold to American, sent to Arizona desert."

"Of course!" Little Ben said, looking up from the papers spread across his lap. "They dismantled a beautiful Victorian stone bridge and replaced it with an ugly concrete one. It makes perfect sense—if you know they had a magical motivation."

"But what happened to that rogue Egalitarian?" I asked. "And what was his plot?"

"Don't know," Chapel said, disappointment radiating from his face. "Before my time. Those records destroyed. Don't even know name of hero who stopped him."

"I do," Dasra said. "It was Lady Roslyn Hill-Haverstock."

Little Ben looked at Dasra in amazement. I looked at Dasra in amazement. Mom and Chapel looked at Dasra in amazement. Only Hungerford seemed unsurprised.

"Now there, there's, there's a name I haven't heard in yonks," he rumbled. "A fine, fine woman she was."

"You know my grandmother?"

"You're, you're Lady Roslyn's grandson? A pleasure to,

to make your acquaintance." Hungerford extended a massive paw, and they shook. "I was by her side in, in, in 1969, when she foiled the nefarious plot against the bridge. What's she, she up to nowadays?"

"Um, let's save that for later," I said. "Let's start with: I can't believe Lady Roslyn was a hero."

"I knew it all along," Mom said. "Didn't I tell you, 'Lady Roslyn is lovely'?"

"You probably did, Mom, but I think that was before she tried to kill you. You're terrified of her now, remember?"

"That's what I said, dear. I can't believe Lady Roslyn was a hero."

"I don't see why it's such a big surprise," Dasra said. "The anarchists have always been troublemakers. You know Guy Fawkes was one of them, right? And the Inheritors of Order have always stood for . . . well, order. My grandmother wouldn't tell me too much, but I do know somebody discovered that London Bridge was the key to retrieving an incredibly valuable artifact. And the only people with knowledge to stop him were my grandmother and—"

He stopped and looked at me intently, as if making a final decision about whether he could trust me. Finally, he went on. "—and Jeremiah Champney."

That didn't quite add up. "The historian? But he doesn't believe in magic."

"He didn't then, either. My grandmother consulted with him but let him believe she was just researching folklore.

After it was done, she thought it best to drop out of touch with him—if he knew too much, he'd be a danger to himself and others. When she heard someone was stealing stones, she thought he might be at risk, and she sent me to keep an eye on him. That turned out to be fortunate, as you saw."

I thought back to that morning in Mr. Champney's office. "Minnie Tickle wasn't escaping with you. She was chasing you."

Dasra nodded. "I believe this is the part where you apologize for misjudging me."

"But I didn't—okay, I *did*, but I had good reason. I mean, your grandmother—"

He smiled triumphantly. "So you *do* judge people by their ancestry."

I sighed. "Fine. I'm sorry."

"We agree, then," Dasra said. "The next step is to report back to my grandmother and see what she wants us to do."

"We do *not* agree," I told him. "I won't judge you for your grandmother's actions, but I sure as heck judge *her* for them. Maybe she was on the side of good a few decades ago, but she isn't now. Fortunately, we have somebody here who can tell us everything she could. Right, Hungerford?"

"Erm, well, the thing is, I may have been, been, been moderately sozzled over the course of that adventure and it's all a bit hazy. We, we went to St. Pancras Old Church, and, and, and, and—well, in a nutshell, that's all I recall."

Little Ben looked up from the files in his lap. "Hey, look

at these." He held up two faded drawings. "This one is London Bridge before 1758. It wasn't just a road—there were houses built along the entire length."

"There aren't any houses on Minnie's bridge," I said.

"Right." Little Ben held up the other drawing. "This is London Bridge after they tore all the houses down to speed up traffic. It looks like Minnie's bridge, but there's a difference."

I saw what he meant. "There are alcoves every twenty feet or so, on both sides of the bridge. For people to rest in, I guess, while they were crossing."

"Those aren't on the new bridge," Dasra said, and then corrected himself. "I mean, the old bridge. I mean, the new Old Bridge that Minnie built, next to the old New Bridge."

"So did she leave those alcoves off on purpose?" I asked. "Or has she not had the chance to get them yet? And if so, where are they?"

"Those alcoves look like, like stone. If they are, and they're still in London, one of, of, of Mrs. Coade's noble creations will know where. I'll ask around."

Chapel sighed, looking disappointed. "I'd better look through our archives, too. Might have that information somewhere."

"While you do," I told him, "the rest of us will go to St. Pancras Old Church and see what we can find."

"You're welcome to do that," Dasra said. "I'm going to talk to the brave hero who saved London last time there was a plot involving London Bridge. I'm going to ask how she did it."

"Fine," I said. "Ask her how she tried to kill my mom, while you're at it. And this time, don't let her glasshouse you about it."

Dasra glared at me. I glared at him.

"Um, guys? You may want to look at this." Little Ben pointed at the TV in the corner.

On the screen we saw the Thames, showing the new bridge next to the old one—I mean, the new Old one next to the old New one—well, the point is, it showed both bridges.

Chapel turned up the volume. ". . . still unsure of the motivation behind the bizarre series of events, which began earlier with a battle between security forces and an unknown terrorist organization. Authorities warn that the new struc-ture may be highly dangerous. The public is advised to stay away, and to call the police immediately if they see any of the following suspects."

Five pictures popped up on screen. One showed Min-nie. Her face was framed by the sky, but the photo had been cropped to hide the fact that she was flying.

The other photos showed me, Mom, Dasra, and Little Ben.

Now it wasn't just Brigadier Beale who thought we were Minnie's accomplices. It was the whole country.

PART THREE

CHAPTER 45

$\mathcal{A}$s we climbed down from the Ouroboarus bus, outside the gates of St. Pancras Old Church, we saw two kids squabbling. Something odd happened each time one of them spoke: there was a faint *blurp*, like a little air bubble popping.

"She hit me first!" the boy said. *Blurp.*

"I never hit him at all!" the girl said. *Blurp.*

"If you two don't settle down," their father said, "I'm never buying you ice cream again." *Blurp.*

"Look," Little Ben said, pointing at a sewer grate near their feet. A teeny puff of mist rose up from it with each *blurp*.

"They're lying," I said. "Inspector Sands said the reason ancient stones were scattered around London is to absorb magic. That's why the city doesn't explode, even though people must be fibbing to each other all the time. But Minnie stole the stones and smashed them. And now if people tell a lie when they aren't quite close enough to a river to cause an explosion, you get that mist."

"Oooh!" Little Ben said, bouncing up and down with excitement. "That's where London fog comes from. And that must be why there hasn't been a huge, thick fog here for decades. They must have fine-tuned the location of the stones or something."

By now, thanks to all the pointing and leaping-in-excitement we were doing, the family was staring at us. Remembering that we were wanted terrorists, I checked my wig, and I saw Little Ben make sure that his rather unconvincing fake mustache was still above his lip. Chapel had managed to dig up a few musty costumes from the Brethren's supplies, and they were only slightly more plausible than Oaroboarus's bus outfit.

We hurried into the churchyard, leaving the family behind. Meanwhile, Oaroboarus made a series of not-very-convincing beeping noises as he backed into a bus lane to wait for us.

Surrounding the church was a large graveyard, complete with grass and tall trees and a dozen stone crypts. It was missing only one thing. "Doesn't a graveyard usually have, you know, gravestones?" I asked.

We found them beneath the leafy branches of a tall ash tree. In tight concentric circles around its trunk, a hundred headstones clustered. Some of them were sunk three-quarters deep in the dirt, with the tree's thick roots gnarled over and between.

"Did they all die at the same time?" Little Ben asked. "Could it be a plague pit?"

"I can't make out most of the dates," I said. The words and numbers had been faded by the years. Some of the stones had been worn completely smooth, while others were partly or even fully legible.

Little Ben gazed intently at one of the headstones. "This one," he murmured, unusually subdued. "There's something about it. It makes me feel . . . I dunno, *sad*."

I looked more closely at it. Whatever carvings had been there were almost completely worn away, but when I ran my hand over them, I could feel a slight indentation. "Do you have pencil and paper?" I asked.

Little Ben tore his eyes away from the headstone and rummaged through his carpetbag. He pulled out a small stub of pencil and a huge square of paper and handed them to me.

I held the paper over the headstone, rubbing the pencil back and forth, and gradually a name took shape:

William Franklin.

"Why does that name sound so familiar?" Little Ben asked. He reached out to touch the gravestone . . .

. . . and it erupted with light, the letters of the tombstone suddenly vivid and clear:

In Memory of
William Franklin,
patriot,
who departed this world
17 November 1813,
in the 82nd year of his life.

Little Ben gasped but didn't draw back. The light dimmed until only the *a* in *Franklin* glowed. Then the *a* blinked out, and the light shot around the circle, leaping from letter to letter, gravestone to gravestone, arriving back at the *a* in *Franklin,* only to continue circling, again and again.

"I think it's spelling something," I said, "but it's too fast to read."

"I wonder . . . ," Little Ben said, and slid his hand to a different spot on the gravestone. As he did, the glowing circle sped up. "Oops. Let's try the other direction." He slid his hand back, and the circle gradually slowed down until we could make out the letters.

"A . . . N . . . S . . . W . . . E . . . R . . . T . . . H . . . E . . . P . . . H . . . O . . . N . . . E," I read. "But where are we going to find a phone in a graveyard?"

"There," Little Ben said, pointing to a crypt on the other side of the tree. It was a tall rectangle, with a curved roof, and now that I thought about it, it did look an awful lot like a carved stone version of the red telephone booths that dotted London. And as we approached it, we could make out a faint ringing sound coming from within.

I ran my hand over the monument, but I couldn't find any way of opening it. "How do we get in?"

Little Ben reached out, and the moment he touched it, a heavy stone block swung open. Inside was an old-fashioned telephone. Now that nothing was blocking it, the ring was deafening.

"Looks like it's for you," I shouted over the noise. "You'd better answer it."

$\mathcal{H}$e picked up the handset and we all put our ears to it.

"Hello?" Little Ben said.

"Hello," answered the distant, scratchy voice of a man. I couldn't place his accent, but it sounded more American than English to me.

"Who is—" Little Ben began, but the voice didn't stop.

"If this message reached you," the voice continued, "it is thanks to the combined scientific and magical ingenuity of myself and my friend John Soane."

"I think it's a recording," I whispered.

"We have learned how to use the rivers of this city to grant immortality—but the process unleashes a terrible danger. In time, we might be able to preserve life—or even to create it from nothing—without this cost. Our research may aid mankind, and we must not destroy it; yet it may prove a catastrophe, and we must not let it fall into the wrong hands. Thus, we shall place a history of our achievements in a place that shall be reachable only by the worthy.

"But who *are* the worthy? There is some disagreement among us. I believe merit must be earned by an individual's actions; John believes it may be inherited. We have therefore agreed on a compromise—a sort of lock with two keys. The first key is this system of communication, which may only be used by us and our descendants. The second key is the hiding place this message shall guide you to. It can only be reached by the right of a free man, earned by one's own labor.

"If you are hearing this, you must be my flesh and blood, or the flesh and blood of my close friends. I therefore send you my greetings from across the ages, and urge you to act with wisdom and prudence.

"I remain, yours truly, Benjamin Franklin."

The message faded out.

"*The* Benjamin Franklin?" I said.

"It would make sense," Little Ben said. "I mean, as much as magic ever makes sense." He started off slowly and thoughtfully, growing more excited as he went along. "Franklin was born in America, but he lived in London for sixteen years. Plus there's my name. Plus he was a printer, and there's a massive printing press in my underground lair! Plus there was a lot about Ben Franklin in my dad's files!! Plus I felt sad about William Franklin's gravestone, and based on the dates, he could have been Benjamin Franklin's son, and maybe the reason I could get the message is that William was my ancestor!!! Maybe I'm Ben Franklin's great-great-great-great-great-great-great-grandson!!!!"

"There's another possibility," I said. "Oaroboarus told me there used to be an old man in your lair. What if Ben Franklin made himself immortal, and that old man was Ben Franklin himself? And Oaroboarus never saw you as a baby—he found you there, already a kid. What if Franklin was right, and whatever he had figured out about the rivers, it let him create life as well as preserve it? What if he had been working on it for hundreds of years, and finally he made you from scratch? That would be why you don't remember anything from the past—you don't have a past to remember."

"Ooooooooooooooooooooooh," Little Ben said. It was the longest "oooh" I had ever heard him say. *"That would be the coolest thing ever."*

"The part about *you* is cool, but if this is tied in to whatever's happening with London Bridge, then Minnie Tickle may be after the secret of life and death itself. And if she—" I began, but Little Ben was too excited to listen.

"Do you think he made me a normal kid, or do you think he gave me superpowers?"

"I don't know—"

"Maybe that's why I can speak so many languages. Maybe I'm Language-Man! Oooh, Ben Franklin was big on lightning. Do you think he used lightning to bring me to life? Am I the fruit of dangerous scientific knowledge, shocked into existence by a mighty storm? Maybe I've got lightning powers! *Kra-kow!*" He pointed at a nearby tree. Nothing happened to it. He pointed harder. It failed to burst into flames. "Aw, man."

"It's probably just as well," I said. "You don't want to go burning down forests every time you sneeze."

"EXCUSE ME, FELLOW PASSERBY," a voice said, loudly. I turned around and spotted an extremely tall woman wrapped in a cloak, her face shadowed by a hood. "IT IS A PERFECTLY NORMAL THING FOR TWO PEOPLE TO CONVERSE," she said in the same loud voice. Then she leaned forwards, so that I could see under her hood. She was made of stone, with a strong, broad face, and the top of her head was flat, as if it usually supported a roof. Underneath her real cloth robe, she was carved to look as though she were wearing Greek clothes. "I'm not actually human," she whispered. "I'm a Coade stone caryatid."

"I gathered," I whispered back.

"Hungerford sent me. This church doesn't have any Coade stones, so he contacted me on the stone network and asked me to sneak over from my church a few blocks away. Do you think anybody noticed?"

The graveyard was mostly empty, and the few other visitors were looking the other way. Either they hadn't heard her shouting, or they *had* heard it and were trying to ignore the crazy woman. "I think you're good," I told her.

"Wonderful," she whispered. "SHALL WE HAVE A CASUAL CONVERSATION?" she shouted, then kept alternating between loud and quiet. "Hungerford says there were four alcoves from the bridge still in London. IT IS A LOVELY DAY AND THE WEATHER IS UNREMARKABLE. Two of them were taken already. I EXPRESS FOND WISHES FOR THE SUCCESS OF YOUR CHOSEN FOOTBALL TEAM."

People were starting to notice us and edge away. She was probably being as subtle as an eight-foot-tall statue could be, so I didn't bother trying to hush her. Instead, I did my best to move her along. "That leaves two alcoves?"

"That's right. I FEEL FAVORABLY TOWARDS DOGS AND HUMAN INFANTS. Both alcoves are in Victoria Park. He's spoken to Chapel Lock and they'll meet you there. I AM SUPPORT PERSONNEL IN A CHURCH PROFESSION. TELL ME OF YOUR OWN OCCUPATION. This subterfuge is exhilarating! I'm going to have to try it more often. Do you have any missions for me? HA HA HA I EXPRESS AMUSEMENT AT YOUR WITTICISM!"

"Not right now," I said. "Why don't you go back to your building and, um, stay alert for suspicious activity. Maybe, you know, try to be quiet. To help with the subterfuge."

"Good plan," she whispered, winking. "Quiet. Subtle. Practically invisible!" She strode away on her massive legs, then paused and waved her arm in a huge, stiff gesture that could be seen from miles away. "FOND REGARDS TO YOUR BELOVED RELATIVES!"

CHAPTER 47

$\mathcal{V}$ictoria Park was a train ride away, and the closer we got, the thicker the fog became. This was a good thing, since Oaroboarus ran behind us the entire way, and his train costume was even less convincing than his bus costume. Not that I could criticize him—I was impressed that he and Little Ben had prepared for all eventualities. They had created an entire old-fashioned steam train from scraps, with a grille on the front made from a rusty drying rack and a working smokestack made from a teakettle puffing out steam. Let's just say it was the kind of costume that became more convincing the less you could see of it.

Fortunately, by the time we stepped out of the station, the fog had gotten so thick that you couldn't see more than a block away.

Little Ben swapped Oaroboarus's train costume for his bus one. "Do you think the fog is thicker everywhere, or just here?"

"I don't know," I said. "And look, it's moving. How does it do that with no breeze?"

As we walked down the ramp from the station to the road, billows of fog flowed alongside us. And as we walked along the road towards the park, they continued to tag along.

"Maybe the fog is going to the park, too," Mom said.

"Mom, come on. That's . . . actually, that might be right." And it was. The fog flowed straight alongside us until we got to the park, at which point, the misty stream turned left along a tree-lined avenue, joining an already thick mass. We stepped into it, and everything vanished. I held up my hand and could see only the faintest outlines of my fingers through the dense, damp mist.

"Wow!" Little Ben's voice said from somewhere nearby. "An authentic London Particular! Back in Victorian times, they were so thick, people used to walk right into the Thames."

Now that we were inside it, I could see swirls of color in the whiteness. A yellow patch twisted past me, and I thought I heard a faint voice murmuring, "Yes, boss, that's a great idea." A black spot whisked past, and I heard, "*She's* been stealing your crayons, not me."

"I think all the lies in London are heading to this park," I said. "Keep walking straight. Let's see if we can get through this."

Holding my arms out in front of me, I maneuvered

around a tree. I emerged onto a large field that was fog-free but goalpost-heavy. I counted six soccer pitches in a row. "Who plays that much soccer?" I asked.

"Here in England, we call it football," Mom said.

"I can call it either!" Little Ben said, bouncing up and down. "I have joint citizenship! I'm a descendant and/or scientific creation of Ben Franklin! Probably!"

The trees ran all the way around the field, and an impenetrable avenue of fog ran all the way around the trees. It was as though everything on the other side of the trees had simply been erased.

"Over here!" a familiar brusque voice called from somewhere in the foggy area.

"Chapel, is that you?" I said. "Keep calling, and we'll find you."

"Not much for talking without purpose. Wait. I know. Battle cry. *Enn brauzt bryggjur Lundúna. Yggs veðrþorinn éla kennir,*" he called loudly.

If his aim was to get us moving towards him, he failed, because I stopped dead in my tracks.

"*Enn brauzt bryggjur Lundúna. Yggs veðrþorinn éla kennir,*" Chapel shouted again, and I got moving, because his battle cry had raised a question that I needed answered. By the fourth or fifth time he was through it, we had stumbled close enough that we could make out his face.

Hungerford trotted up, apparently guided through the fog by Chapel's voice as well.

"Where did you hear those words?" I asked Chapel.

"Don't know meaning. Old Brethren fight song. Never paid much attention to translations. About a battle on London Bridge. Viking? Anglo-Saxon? Not sure."

"Little Ben, did you understand it?"

"No! That's the first language I've found that I don't speak," Little Ben said. "Why do you ask?"

"Because those are the words to a family lullaby. My mom and my aunts have been singing it to me since I was little. Only they sing it slower and . . . sillier, I guess."

I sang the words I had tapped out to Mom when we were locked in cells next to each other: *"Ann browsed bridger luna doona, Eggs feather thorn, a la kenner."*

Mom joined in—and through the fog, other voices echoed us. "This way," I said, and we stumbled towards the voices.

As the echoes faded, a stone archway emerged through the fog. We stepped inside it, and suddenly, we could see each other. The fog stayed outside, as though held back by an invisible wall.

We were in a small stone alcove, about twice as tall as I was. "Is this an alcove from Old London Bridge?" Little Ben asked.

"Look up," Chapel answered, pointing upwards to a symbol etched in the very top of the arch. It was a triangle overlaid on an X overlaid on a circle, with a cross on top. "Bridge Mark. Symbol of the Brethren."

I thought back to the zombie bunny rabbit that Lady Roslyn wore around her neck, which had turned out to be an illustration of the first urn that carried water. "Is it a symbol or a rune? I mean, does it have magic powers?"

"Not sure," Chapel said, although his face had already said it. "Good question. Wish I'd asked. Only know it's on everything the Brethren built."

I tried to make sense of it all. "My ancestors were caretakers of the secret rivers, and the Brethren were caretakers of the bridge that harnessed their powers. Maybe that's why we know the same song."

"When you sang it from a distance, the alcove echoed it," Little Ben said. "What happens if you try it from inside the alcove?"

"Ann browsed bridger luna doona," Mom and I sang. *"Eggs feather thorn, u lu kenner."*

"BAAAA," somebody said. I looked at Hungerford in astonishment.

"Don't, don't direct your attention in my direction," he said. "That's not the, the, the sound typically associated with my species."

"BAAAAA." It was definitely a sheep, somewhere nearby.

Little Ben's eyes opened in a sudden realization. "It's the other alcoves," he said. "People used to stand in one alcove on London Bridge and whisper, and people in other alcoves could hear them. They thought it was the shape of the stone that focused the echoes—but it must have been magic. And I think you've reactivated it."

"So there are sheep wandering into the other alcoves somewhere?" I said. "Why sheep?"

"Why don't we ask her?" Mom said.

"What are you talking about, Mom?"

"Well, if we can hear the sheep, they can hear us, right? So we'll wait until Minnie shows up to pet the sheep, and then we can ask her where she is."

"That's the most ridiculous—" I stopped and switched to a whisper. "You're right. I mean, kind of. If we can hear the sheep, Minnie can hear us. If she shows up at the other alcoves, wherever they are, we can eavesdrop on her. But we'd better be quiet."

We didn't have long to wait. After a few peaceful minutes, listening to the sheep bleating and the lies murmuring through the mist, we jumped when a raspy voice croaked out, "Drop me off here, Dad."

Was that Minnie? She sounded like an old woman with a bad cigarette habit. Whoever it was paused, as if listening to somebody else, then continued, "I'll meet you at the London Stone once I've—"

Her voice faded out. She must have stepped out of her alcove.

I walked out of ours, gesturing to the others to follow me. Back out in the fog, we couldn't see each other, but at least we could talk without fear of being overheard.

Little Ben spoke first. "If they're going after the London Stone, it's even worse than we thought. That's the most ancient and powerful stone in the city. It's—"

I held up a hand to interrupt him, then realized he wouldn't be able to see it. Heck, *I* couldn't see it. So I interrupted the slightly less polite way. "Stop! Listen."

Over the sheep and the lies, we heard the sound of a motor.

"I bet that's the Precious Man's van," I said. "They'll be here any minute."

CHAPTER 48

"*L*et's hide and see what she does," Little Ben said.

"Hide? Nonsense. Time for battle," Chapel said. With his expressive face hidden by the fog, his tone of voice seemed even brusquer.

"Chapel's right," I said. "It's not like we can get those stolen stones back anymore. Plus, I think I know why she's here. Follow me."

Then after a pause, I added, "Specifically, follow me to the soccer fields, which is where you'd see me heading, if you could see me."

I felt my way to the inside of the foggy wall, away from the road. When the others had emerged, I gestured to the field around us.

"Why isn't the fog collecting here? What makes this

area unique? It's all those goalposts. And goalposts are big pieces of metal with nets hung over them. I know from personal experience that the right kind of metal, arranged in the right way, can control magic. It's true of faucets and I bet it's true of goalposts, too. I bet you anything those goalposts and the stone alcoves were part of whatever defense system the city had set up with the stones, to prevent explosions. And now that the stones are gone, the fog is pouring into the park and hovering around the edges of this magical circuit."

"So what do we do?" Little Ben asked.

"Chapel, you head to the London Stone and capture the Precious Man."

Delight spread across his face, mixed with a hunger for action, but all he said was "Right." He ran off into the fog

"As for us," I said, "we're going to—"

That's when Minnie Tickle flew out of the fog. She had beams shooting out of both hands, each one levitating an alcove. She did not look happy to see us.

So I just yelled "DESTROY THE GOALS!" and ran towards the nearest one.

Now, I had read plenty of articles about fans tearing down goalposts after a game, and I had always imagined it was the kind of thing that happened in one excited instant. It turned out that pulling over a massive piece of metal embedded in concrete wasn't an easy task. I jumped and I pulled. Nothing happened. Seconds later, Little Ben got there and started jumping and pulling. Nothing happened.

Oaroboarus head-butted it repeatedly. That was a lot noisier, but not much more effective.

Meanwhile, Minnie had spread her arms, making the hovering alcoves fly towards opposite ends of the field. Her tattoos began to swirl. Beams shot out of her fingers, and as she slowly closed her arms, the beams closed in, too, sweeping the London Particular up between them, as though each beam were an alcove-tipped tong. The fog didn't breach the invisible wall that seemed to stretch between the goalposts, but that wall must not have gone very high. The fog began to collect over our heads.

"Stand aside!" Hungerford roared as he ran headfirst into the goal. It probably would have been better if he had roared it *before* he ran into the goal, since that might have given us humans time to get out of the way. Still, even though the falling goal smashed me and Little Ben to the ground, I couldn't complain too much. Hungerford had gotten the job done.

And now that the goal was down, the fog above us began to wobble inside the beams of light, like soup sloshing in a bowl. But it didn't spill out.

Minnie now faced a dilemma. To aim a lightning bolt at us, she'd have to point her hands, but that would mean losing even more control of the fog.

She let the alcoves fall, pointed both hands at Hungerford, and fired.

As Hungerford staggered back, the fog began billowing away. Minnie quickly turned her attention back to it. Fresh beams shot out, catching the alcoves moments before they hit the ground.

"Are you okay?" I asked.

"I'm, I'm, I'm winded but entirely undaunted," he said, but there was a scorch mark on his side where she had hit him, and some of his stone flesh had been chipped away.

"Hungerford's the only one of us who can knock these goals down," I said, "but I don't know how many more hits he can take. So the rest of us are going to—"

Before I could finish, Oaroboarus ran towards the nearest goal and began head-butting it futilely. I knew he wasn't going to knock it over, but I also knew better than to waste time trying to stop him. So I turned to the others. "The rest of us except Oaroboarus are going to do everything we can to draw Minnie's fire while he knocks down more goals."

"NONSENSE!" roared Hungerford. "I refuse to, to, to permit my allies to absorb the blows intended for—"

"It's the strategically sound choice," I said. "CHARGE!"

Little Ben and I ran straight for Minnie.

Mom did not. She had somehow gotten fascinated by a particular curved piece of broken goalpost, and she crouched down on the grass, fiddling with it. I was annoyed, but if it meant she wasn't going to get in my way, it was probably a good decision.

Hungerford charged after us, which was *not* a good decision. Apparently strategic soundness was not the way to convince him. I tried another approach. "Down with the goalposts! For the honor of Mrs. Coade!"

"For Mrs. Coade!" he roared, and split off.

As Little Ben and I came at her, Minnie fired lightning bolts, dropping one hand to shoot, then once again pointing it up to catch the falling alcove, and then dropping the other hand to shoot again. She looked like she was conducting a symphony and juggling at the same time. It was an impressive performance, but I was too busy trying not to die to appreciate it. Fortunately, with the three of us weaving towards her, her aim wasn't as keen as it might have been. She singed my heels and my elbow, and I got at least two fireball haircuts, but we managed to get down to her end of the field without major injury.

Once we were there, we had a bit of a problem:

When you're fighting an opponent who can fly, all she has to do is go up a couple of feet in the air, and she's out of your reach.

And when she can throw fireballs, it doesn't matter how high she goes: *you're* still in *her* range.

"Run away!" I said, and we turned around and started weaving back.

Hey, I hadn't actually expected to stop her. All I wanted to do was give her enough to worry about that she wouldn't focus on Hungerford while he knocked down more goals. And I could see that he had toppled three more. That left eight, including the one that Oaroboarus was still head-butting to no effect whatsoever.

Singed but still alive, I made it back to where Mom was standing. She had finally finished fiddling with the bent goalpost fragment, and she held it up right in front of my face. "Look, dear! I put some torn-up net on it so it looks like a flower!"

"Mom, that's not import—"

I was interrupted by a fireball shot straight at my face.

$\mathcal{T}$he fireball went right into Mom's homemade flower. The net caught it, and it stayed there, fizzing, close enough that I could feel how badly it would have burned me if Mom hadn't stopped it.

I had to admit: the ball of flame, spinning in the torn lace of the net, reflecting off the metal of the broken bit of goalpost—it was beautiful, even if it looked less like a flower and more like an incandescent soccer ball.

Soccer ball. Huh.

"Drop that for me, would you, Mom?"

She let go. As it fell towards the ground, I had a moment of doubt. The fact that the fireball was staying inside Mom's makeshift container suggested that the particular combination of metal and lace had some kind of holding powers. So if

I kicked it, it *probably* wouldn't burn my foot to a cinder. But that was a pretty wobbly probably.

Fortunately, I only had a second to think, which wasn't long enough to reach an intelligent conclusion, so instead, I did the dumb thing. I kicked it.

My foot did not explode. It smashed into the fireball, sending it flying out of the net flower and towards Minnie. She ducked.

"Mom, can you make more of these?"

"Sure, honey! I'm so glad you like them!"

I picked up the one she had already made and ran towards Minnie, who had recovered enough to fire another ball at me. I caught it in the net, drop-kicked it, and shot it back.

This time, Minnie was ready, and she dodged it easily, but I didn't care. While I had kept her busy, Hungerford had knocked down two more goals. That left six.

The fog was shaking like Jell-O in an earthquake. Some of it sloshed over the side of Minnie's magic light box and floated away.

And Mom had finished another flower. Little Ben ran over to her. In an attempt to stop him, Minnie shot a fireball, but she was a moment too late. Little Ben grabbed the flower and caught the fireball just in time. Then he punched the net and sent it flying right at Minnie, who dodged it again.

"Little Ben! Go long!" I grabbed a fireball, passed it to Ben, and dodged another shot.

Hungerford had knocked down two more goals. Four to go.

"Go right! Catch! Shoot!"

Two goals to go.

I caught a fireball, punched it to Little Ben, caught another one, and kicked it at Minnie, so that it crackled at her from one side while Little Ben's came from the other. She dropped down, letting the fireballs collide above her head.

One goal to go. Instead of head-butting it, Oaroboarus was attacking it with his tusks. That wasn't working any better, but for him, it showed a certain degree of flexibility.

Minnie hurled balls at us faster than ever. *WHOOSH!* I caught one. *WHOOSH!* Before I could send it back, another one smacked into my net, doubling the size of the fireball already there. *WHOOSH! WHOOSH! WHOOSH!* The ball in my net was now so bright I could barely look at it, and so hot I had to hold it at arm's length.

Minnie let out a hoarse scream of frustration. All she said was "AAAAAAIIGH," but it was enough for me to confirm that the scratchy voice we had heard before was hers.

I punched my multi-fireball at her. As soon as it left the net, it expanded into something as big as a Hula-Hoop. And as it approached Minnie, her expression turned from fury to terror. She could have dodged it easily, but she froze, clearly panicked. *It's going to kill her,* I thought.

I wasn't her biggest fan—I tend to reserve my fandom for people who did not commit crimes against creativity and then leave me to take the blame. But I didn't want to kill anybody. So I yelled, "MOVE, Minnie! MOVE!"

That snapped her out of it. She lurched to the side, and

the huge fireball brushed past her. She would have escaped singe-free, but her awkward lurch made the loose end of her scarf belt fly up, right into the fireball's path.

Her belt caught fire.

She screamed that hoarse scream of hers and yanked her belt off, throwing it to the ground.

Then she looked at me, hatred in her eyes.

She lifted both hands and pointed them at me. Her tattoos swirled and glowed.

CHAPTER 50

$\mathcal{I}$ didn't know what she was going to do to me, but I didn't think it was going to be pretty. "I just saved your life," I called.

She hesitated.

And as she did, Hungerford sent the last goal (and Oaroboarus) toppling to the ground. The fog tumbled outwards.

Maybe my words swayed Minnie, or maybe she ran out of time. Either way, instead of blowing me up, she gave me one last dirty look, then scooped up both alcoves and as much fog as she could catch and flew up, disappearing out of sight.

"She's heading west," Little Ben said, "towards the London Stone. We've got to get there before her."

"No, we don't," murmured a voice at my waist. I glanced down.

I was still holding the flower Mom had made out of bent metal and net, and a little bit of fog had gotten caught up in it. "There's really no urgency," the fog murmured.

I shook the lie out of the net. It floated down and curled around my ankle. I shooed it away and turned to Little Ben. "How can we beat her? She can fly."

"There is one, one, one suitably expedient pathway," Hungerford said, pounding a manhole cover with his paw. It flipped back, revealing a tunnel that should have been leading down, but somehow led sideways.

"Let's go!" Little Ben cried, and leapt down—I mean, left—I mean, leftrightish—anyway, he jumped through the manhole.

I opened my mouth to explain why we didn't really need to take the Coadeway, but no good explanation came out, so I shut it and jumped in whatever direction counted as *in*.

As my feet hit the ground, wall, ceiling, or whatever it was that I landed on, Hungerford and Mom landed next to me.

Hungerford trotted off. I focused my eyes on his tail and tried to block out everything else. "Little Ben, tell me about the London Stone. It might be useful." *And distracting,* I added mentally.

"It's been sitting on the same street in London for thousands of years. Nobody knows what it is. Maybe it's the very first stone the Romans laid when they built Londinium! Maybe it's the rock from which King Arthur pulled Excalibur!"

"The London Stone was a giant's toothbrush," a voice at my ankle murmured. That little bit of lying fog was there, rubbing up against my leg and purring.

I kicked it, but my leg passed right through it. "Shoo! Get out of here!" I said. It gave a hurt sniff and drifted off. "If it really is the first stone ever laid in London," I continued, "it's had longer than any other to absorb magic. It would be the most powerful object in the city. Why would Minnie wait until now to grab it?"

"Ooh, good question. Maybe it was *too* powerful for her to handle until she had control over all the other stones. Or maybe . . ."

He hesitated.

"Go on!" I said. "If you stop talking, I'll have to look at the walls."

"Well, there's an old saying: 'As long as the London Stone stands, so too shall London.' What if that's true? What if the city will collapse when she steals it? Maybe she and the Precious Man needed to be sure they could make their getaway before that happens."

I nodded. Then I stopped nodding, because moving my head up and down reminded me that "up" and "down" weren't behaving the way I expected them to. Instead, I said, "If the London Stone is the final thing they need, then this is our last chance. She's ready to 'exercise the right of a free man,' whatever that means."

"I've got it!" Mom said. "I had a personal trainer named Mr. Freeman. Maybe she's going to exercise with him."

"That's it!" Little Ben said.

"It is?" I asked.

"Kind of. Ben Franklin wasn't talking about a free man. He was talking about a Freeman, one word. If London considers somebody particularly worthy, it grants that person the Freedom of the City. Nowadays, it's mostly ceremonial, but Freemen have certain ancient rights. Like, if they're sentenced to death, they can demand to be hanged with a silk rope. And the most famous one is: they have the right to drive sheep across London Bridge."

Suddenly, the BAA-ing made sense. "Wool soaks up water and keeps you warm even when it's wet. In a city of magical rivers, umbrellas are powerful because they control water. Maybe it's the same principle with wool."

Hungerford placed his paw on a parallelogram-shaped door on the floor and swung it open. "Cannon Street station," he said. "Alight here for, for the London Stone. You good people go on. I'm going to, to, to hang back out of sight."

Hungerford was learning to be discreet? That was almost as disorienting as the Coadeway itself. We hopped down through the door. Gravity bent at ninety degrees, and we found ourselves standing on the pavement.

CHAPTER 51

We stood there, breathing in the straight lines and right angles. And there were a lot of them to appreciate. Cannon Street station was a big, boxy glass building, covered from the first floor upwards with a frame of interlocking metal bars that made it look like it was being held inside a giant cage.

We crossed the street to where Chapel stood guard next to the most powerful magical stone in London. Stop for a moment and picture it: an ancient and mysterious object, heavy with millennia of enchantment. Can you imagine its glory, and the splendor of its case, and the reverence the passersby would show for it?

Well, if you can, you're imagining it wrong.

Now try picturing a small hunk of rock barely visible behind a scratched piece of glass protected by a dinged-up iron railing with chipped paint, low on the wall of an ugly 1960s office building, going entirely unnoticed by the crowds hurrying past. If you've got that image firmly in mind, you'll know exactly what we were seeing.

"That's it?" I asked. *"That's* the stone from which Arthur drew Excalibur?"

"Yeah!" Little Ben said. "Isn't it *amazing?"*

"That's one word for it."

"It's a much less popular sight than it used to be," Mom said.

"Than it used to be when you were a kid?"

"No, than it used to be thirty seconds ago," Mom said. "It's so nice that we finally have it all to ourselves."

She was right. Formerly crowded with pedestrians, the sidewalk was suddenly clear. For that matter, the constant noise of passing traffic had stopped, too. I looked up from the stone and discovered why.

At both ends of the block, the intersections were filled with tanks and soldiers with guns. Around the edges of the blockade, military police in riot gear stood with linked arms, keeping the crowd back. Underneath the helmets and the face shields, all the personnel had a familiar orange pockmarked look.

Atop one of the tanks stood Brigadier Beale, holding a megaphone. "Step away from the stone," he said. "We've got you surrounded."

"Don't be crazy," I called back. "Minnie Tickle's going to be here any minute."

"And how would you know that," he megaphoned, "if you weren't with her?"

"Because while you've been shooting at things, we've been investigating. She's—"

"Five," Brigadier Beale said.

I pressed on. "She's got all the alcoves now and—"

"Four," Brigadier Beale said.

"—she's got sheep, and—"

"Three," Brigadier Beale said.

"Hyacinth . . . ," Little Ben said.

I ignored him. "And she's after—"

"Two."

"HYACINTH!" Little Ben hissed. "Those are regular tanks and guns. They're not the pebble-shooting kind. We do NOT want him to get to—"

"One."

"We surrender," I said, stepping back with my hands in the air. Little Ben and Chapel did the same.

Only Mom stood there, gazing at Brigadier Beale with the same detached look she had aimed at the broken bits of goalpost metal. "He hasn't tied his shoes very carefully," she said. "You should never go into battle with loose shoelaces."

I lowered my hands long enough to yank Mom away from the London Stone. "She surrenders, too."

"Excellent choice," Beale said. "Take them into custody."

Led by Beale, a group of Corkers approached us. Some of them had handcuffs, but one of them had what looked like a large torture device. As he got closer, he squeezed a trigger on it, and it roared to life.

Chapel's face clouded with the thunderous fury of chivalry insulted. "Probably shouldn't torture people who surrendered," he said mildly.

"It's not for you, mate," said the Corker who was carrying it. It was the first time I had heard a Corker say anything other than *Pop!*, and now that I came to think of it, he looked trim and fit in his uniform, rather than massive and hulking. He must have been not a Corker but a human—but unlike the others, his face shield was tinted black, stopping me from seeing his face.

Before I could place his voice, Chapel pulled his sword from his crocheted scabbard (shredding it yet again) and smashed the flat edge of his blade into the torture device, sending it crashing to the ground.

The black-masked non Corker jumped back out of the way as a mob of actual Corkers bounded in.

"*Enn brauzt bryggjur Lundúna,*" Chapel yelled. He leapt into the air and, in a single whirling strike, sliced off a dozen cork arms as they extended to grab him. He landed on a Corker's head and bounced up with a *sproing*, somersaulting onto a second-story window ledge.

He might not have been much of a talker, but he was awfully impressive as a fighter.

Undeterred by the loss of their arms, the Corkers swarmed together into a pyramid, rising up to Chapel's height. As they rose, they swelled together, forming a single mass of cork. It flowed over Chapel until only his head was visible, and then flowed off, carrying him away. Every muscle on his face strained with effort as he struggled to escape, but all he said, quietly, was "Bother."

When he was gone, the human Corker bent down and picked up his torture device. He carried it to the iron grille in front of the London Stone, pushed the tip of his device into it, and unscrewed the bolts that held it in place.

So it turned out it was less of a torture device and more of an electric screwdriver. I wished Chapel had waited to get all the information before getting himself carted off.

With the iron grating gone, I could finally get a good look at the London Stone, and it was more impressive than I had realized. It was about two feet tall, longer than it was wide, and the top had been carved into a series of purposeful curves—although what that purpose was, I couldn't say. Along the sides, it was rough and uneven and pocked with holes, some as deep as a skeleton's eye sockets. I could feel power emanating from it.

"We've had emergency backup plans in place for years," Beale said as two Corkers lowered the stone into a wheeled cart, "but my supervisor refused to implement them unless there was a theft attempt. Now that you've engaged in one, I can finally move it somewhere safer."

"We are NOT stealing it," I told him. "But Minnie is going to be here any minute. And by taking off the railing that was protecting it, you've only made her job easier."

"He knows that," a voice called from the corner. I looked over to see a fireman trying to break free of the Corker who was holding him back.

No, not a fireman—it was Dasra, wearing the oversized fireman's uniform he had borrowed from the Brethren's office as a disguise. "My grandmother told me the name of the man behind the last plot against London Bridge. It was Valentine Beale, Senior." He pointed at Brigadier Beale. "It was your father."

CHAPTER 52

*B*eale's eyes narrowed. "Bring him here," he said.

"Don't listen to him," Dasra said. "This man is a traitor."

If you were going to make a list of Adults Who Are Most Likely To Take Orders From A Kid, you'd find "military police who have just gotten an entirely different order from a high-ranking officer" pretty close to the bottom. The only thing lower would be "enchanted beings who were probably created with some sort of spell of obedience." So I wasn't very surprised when one of the Corkers grabbed Dasra by the elbows and pushed him over to us.

"Cuff them," Beale said. The Corkers obeyed that order, too.

"You're despicable," Dasra said.

"You'll never get away with this," I said.

"You really should tie your shoe better," Mom said.

Only Little Ben was silent, gazing thoughtfully upwards. He poked me with his elbow and gestured towards the sky with his head. A distant dot was rapidly approaching us, growing bigger all the time. *Minnie.*

"Get these children and their accomplices out of here," Beale said. "We've got work to do."

As one group of Corkers carried the stone across the street, towards Cannon Street station, another dragged us to a police van. They swung open the back doors and were about to throw us in when one of them finally spotted Minnie zooming towards us.

Pop! he yelled, pointing.

Beale spun around and saw her, too. She crashed to the ground in front of the building where the stone had been on display. She didn't have the alcoves anymore; she must have stopped somewhere along the way to drop them off.

"Bulldog one—fire!" Beale yelled. The tank spat smoke and thunder, but flames bloomed from Minnie's fingers, and she blasted out of the way, leaving the tank's shell to crash into the wall, which collapsed into rubble.

"Formations!" Beale yelled, and the Corkers surrounding us ran off to join their comrades.

Of course, when you're battling a girl who has the power to command stones, reducing a building to rubble only gives her more ammunition. Did that mean Dasra was right, and Beale was really in cahoots with Minnie? Or was it just another example of his shoot-first-think-later style?

Either way, it worked out beautifully for Minnie. She whirled her hands and the pile of debris began whirling, too, like the winds of a tornado.

Then she pointed at the Corkers, and the tornado shot towards them, pulverizing tanks and smashing machine-gun placements. We ran, but the Corkers stayed by their weapons—for about three seconds, until the tornado spun them into the air, bouncing off walls as they went.

By now, the group that was carrying the London Stone had made it into Cannon Street station. Beale ran in after them. "Lockdown!" he yelled, and the massive metal cage that surrounded the top floors of the building plummeted down, blocking off the entrance. Minnie pointed, sending the tornado whirling towards it, but no matter how hard the storm of stones crashed against the metal bars, they didn't budge.

Safely inside, Beale yelled, "Gas!"

One of the few Corkers who hadn't been blown away lifted up a riot gun and squeezed the trigger. A canister shot out, hitting the pavement below where Minnie floated. Gas poured out, billowing towards us.

"This way!" I yelled, running in the opposite direction with Little Ben and Mom close on my heels. We turned down a side lane, where that one Corker with a black glass mask was crouched. He ignored us as we ran past.

I peeked back around the corner. Where Minnie had been, all I could see was a massive white cloud of smoke. In moments, it was going to reach us.

"You don't have a gas mask in that carpetbag, do you?" I asked Little Ben. He shook his head.

"You don't need one," a voice at my ankle murmured. The little patch of lying fog was back.

Great. Just what I needed.

Wait: maybe it *was* what I needed.

I reached down with my still-cuffed hands and scratched the fog like I would a cat, although usually when I scratched cats, my fingers didn't pass right through them. Still, the fog purred.

"There's a big cloud coming our way," I said. "Do you speak tear gas? Can you convince it to leave us alone?"

"Oh, I couldn't possibly do that," the fog whispered. Then it swirled off, right into the billowing mass of gas.

The tear gas stopped in place. It hovered there, billowing white, and then a streak of yellow appeared and began to spread, turning every color of the rainbow as it went.

Then it swept down to us, but now instead of tear gas, it was lie fog. As the multicolored dampness swept past, voices echoed around us: "It wasn't me . . . I meant it in a nice way . . . No, I don't know who broke your vase."

The fog swept past us and vanished into the distance.

"There's an old trick for you," said the soldier crouched nearby. "Using lies to wipe away tears."

He flipped up the glass shield over his face, and I stared at him in disbelief. *"Troy?"* I said.

CHAPTER 53

*N*ewfangled Troy winked at me. "In the flesh. Driving a cab was getting dull. I decided I wanted a job with a little more action. Brigadier Beale doesn't hire too many humans, but I managed to blag my way in."

Troy and Dasra stared at each other, and I knew what was coming next. I was pretty sure Troy liked me as much as I liked him, and seeing me in the company of a cute boy my own age was undoubtedly going to make him jealous. I hoped it wasn't going to be a problem—we had enough to deal with already. I mentally rehearsed the speech I'd give him: *Troy, it's true that Dasra's really cute, and it turns out I hate him less than I thought, but you've got to put aside your feelings and—*

Troy interrupted my thoughts by clapping Dasra on

the shoulder and beaming at him. "Dasra, old boy—funny meeting you here," he said, in an astoundingly posh accent. (Newfangled Troy seemed to switch accents as often as he switched jobs. When I first met him, he was working as a tosher, and he had the same thick accent that the other sewer scavengers did. Then I found him driving a cab and sounding like an ordinary Londoner. One of these days, I was going to figure out which accent was his real one.)

"You know each other?" I asked.

"We met at my father's club," Dasra said, grinning back at Troy. "Great to see you again!"

Troy winked at me over Dasra's shoulder, and I wondered how he had gotten into whatever fancy club Dasra's family belonged to. But all Troy said was "Let's catch up later, shall we?" He pulled a key from his pocket and uncuffed us.

"Are you helping us out of the goodness of your heart?" I asked him. "Or do you smell a profit?"

"What makes you think they're mutually exclusive?" he said. "If Minnie destroys the London Stone—well, let's say there tend to be fewer jobs when all your potential employers have been flattened."

Now that we were all free, Troy pocketed the key and saluted us. "I'd better get back to my battalion before they get suspicious."

"That's it?" I said. "A quick unlock and you're gone?"

"Trust me," he said. "You want me where I can have some influence on where the bullets are going."

"And why's that?"

"Because Minnie just noticed you."

He was right. The tornado was heading right at us, with Minnie floating in the eye.

Minnie glanced down and flicked a finger, and a stream of stones shot towards us.

CHAPTER 54

$\mathscr{I}$'d worn Excalibrolly tucked in my belt ever since I had found it, but I hadn't been any more conscious of it than I was of my own hips. It just felt like a part of me.

But now, without thinking what I was doing, I grabbed it, opened it, and leapt forwards, all in one motion. The stones ricocheted off the umbrella, pinging like hail.

The hail stopped. "On the count of three," I said, "I'm going to close the umbrella. We'll leap for her and try to finish her off. One . . . two . . . three!"

I shut Excalibrolly—revealing Minnie standing right in front of us.

Maybe I should have counted to "One."

She lifted her hand up and a cantaloupe-sized mass of rubble coalesced around her fist.

She swung.

I only had a fraction of a second to react, but I had trained for exactly this circumstance. When I was seven, Aunt Uta had taught me something she described as an "improvised umbrella dance." I held the umbrella, and she led. Depending on what move she made, I had to make various moves in response. If she tried to touch me, I had to block her with the surface of the umbrella. If she did a high kick, I had to catch her ankle with the handle.

We even did a dance show for my mom and all her sisters, with Aunt Polly playing "Singin' in the Rain," and that was fun. But Aunt Uta wouldn't let it rest—for months and months, long after I was bored with the game, she kept drilling me on it.

And so, instinctively, as Minnie's stone-encrusted hand shot towards my chin, I popped open Excalibrolly. It blocked her fist, and I could feel the handle shudder with the impact. I wondered, as I often had lately, how my aunts had known exactly which situations to prepare me for.

Then I stopped wondering and started dancing.

"I'm singin' in the rain," I sang.

I blocked three more punches.

"Doo de dee, dee," I belted. (Aunt Uta hadn't made me practice the words anywhere near as much as the movements.)

Minnie's foot shot towards me in a high kick, stones flying through the air to encrust it as it went. I shut the umbrella, flipped it over, caught her ankle in the crook of the sword handle, and sent her flying.

"Dum dee, dah dee dah. Dee da, dee dah."

She rolled, leapt to her feet, and came towards me, arms swinging wide. I rammed the point of the umbrella into her chest. She toppled over.

I leapt onto her. This was not part of the umbrella dance, by the way. It just seemed like a good idea.

And it *was* a good idea, and I was even smart enough to hold down her wrists so that she couldn't hit me.

Unfortunately, I wasn't smart enough to hold down her fingers. They made a series of rapid magical gestures, and I heard a rumble behind me. I didn't look back, because I wasn't going to fall for the old make-somebody-look-over-their-shoulder-and-then-hit-them trick.

Something grabbed my shoulders and lifted me off the ground, and as I twisted in its grasp, I realized I had instead fallen for the rarer but more deadly create-a-giant-creature-out-of-rubble trick. The thing that held me had massive feet made out of broken bricks, and arms and legs of bent steel girders, and a torso of cracked marble, and a head made out of jagged fragments of window glass. Nearby, Mom and Little Ben dangled from the steel hands of two more rubble monsters.

I swung my umbrella, sending bits of its head flying. The fragments instantly re-coalesced.

It reached over with steel fingers and snatched the umbrella out of my hand, flinging it away.

CHAPTER 55

$\mathcal{J}$ kicked my legs and swung my arms, but the creature was holding me too far away for my fists to reach him—and even if they could have, what use was my soft human flesh going to be against a building personified?

"By Royal Proclamation, We command you to unhand those servants of the Crown," a shrill voice piped up. The rubble monster looked down. There, barely coming up to its ankles, stood Coade stone King George III.

With a slight flick of its leg, the rubble monster kicked George flying. The little king spun through the air, crying "This is treeeeeeeeeeason" right up to the moment he smashed into a traffic light and crashed down . . .

. . . and landed on Hungerford's back. Lined up next to the lion was an army of his Coade stone cousins: elephants and miniature horses and massive Egyptian gods and flowers and urns and sheep, not to mention the tall, flat-headed caryatid, who waved excitedly at me. "THIS IS A SITE OF GENERAL TOURIST INTEREST, AND MY PRESENCE HERE IS PERFECTLY EXPLAINABLE!" she shouted.

Hungerford glared at Minnie. "Prepare to face the, the, the, the . . . Oh, dash it. ROAAAARRRRRR!" He leapt towards her.

Minnie summoned a wall of rubble in front of her. Hungerford smashed into it, bouncing off, and the rubble re-formed into a giant humanoid twice as big as the one that held me. Its massive fist smashed down onto Hungerford and exploded into brick dust, leaving Hungerford unharmed.

"Perhaps you, you were misinformed," Hungerford growled, "but Coade stone is, is vastly stronger than natural rock."

Minnie waved her fingers wildly, filling the streets with flying shards of concrete and smashed bricks, which coalesced into an army of rubble monsters.

The rubble monsters glared at the Coade stone statues.

The Coade stone statues glared at the rubble monsters.

And then the battle began, beautifully carved Coade stone creations against hulking and misshapen humanoids.

"Cry havoc, and let slip the dogs of war!" yelled Coade stone Shakespeare, poking a rubble monster in its glass eyes with his Coade stone quill.

"🏺𝔤† 𝔤 🐦," exclaimed an Egyptian god, hurling a stone lightning bolt.

"I AM FORCED TO ADMIT THAT THIS MAY BE SLIGHTLY UNUSUAL," yelled the caryatid, smashing her flat head into a rubble monster's marble torso.

The ground was soon coated with heaps of pulverized concrete, and Coade stone fish swam through it as naturally as if it were water, sliding under rubble monsters' feet and sending them tumbling.

Like Hungerford had said, the Coade stones were too hard to smash, but most of them were smaller than he was, and without his mass, they were easily sent flying. And when a rubble monster was destroyed, Minnie could wave her hands and it would re-form, although once it reached a certain level of pulverization, she seemed unable to put it back together. The battle was about even, and in the chaos, it took me a moment to realize that Minnie was flying upwards.

She shot to the top floor of Cannon Street station, which had been left unprotected when the metal cage dropped down to cover the entrance. Minnie pointed at a chunk of masonry the size of a compact car, yanking it towards her on a thin rope of fire. She swung the chunk around her head and smashed it into the station's unprotected roof.

She's breaking in, I thought. *But why? If Brigadier Beale is really on her side, couldn't he let her in?*

There was only one way to find out.

"Hungerford!" I yelled. "Get me down from here!"

Hungerford didn't need to be asked twice. He dove

between the steel legs of one rubble monster and bounded through the brick hand of another, pulverizing it into brick dust. Then he launched himself towards the one that held me. Stone shrieked against steel as Hungerford's teeth crumpled against the monster's arm. With a voice that sounded like wind howling through a poorly sealed window, it shrieked in pain and dropped me.

High above, Minnie was still smashing her enchanted wrecking ball against the roof, which looked like it was about to give way. I had to get up there, and quickly. But how? I wasn't going to climb up eight stories, and Hungerford couldn't pull himself up on the metal girders with those clumsy paws of his.

Fortunately, there was someone there with big, strong hands and long enough arms to reach from bar to bar.

"Hey, Carrie!" I called. "CLIMBING IS A COMMON HUMAN SPORT AND ENTIRELY INCONSPICUOUS."

CHAPTER 56

*M*innie gave one last smash with her wrecking ball and the roof of Cannon Street station caved in. She flew in through the gap.

Two stories below, I clung to the caryatid as she pulled herself swiftly upwards. "I've always wanted to do this," she said. "You can't imagine how dull it gets, supporting a building from the bottom. Finally, I'm going to see one from the top. PERHAPS IT IS AN OPTICAL ILLUSION AND PASSERSBY ARE NOT ACTUALLY SEEING A LIVING STATUE IN ACTION."

In a few rapid motions, she pulled us up onto the roof and leapt into the hole.

We plummeted into the wreckage of an office. Fluorescent lights hung limply from the shattered ceiling,

and computer monitors had been cracked and splin-
tered by pieces of plaster. Fortunately, there was no sign
of workers—Beale must have cleared the area before the
battle began.

The caryatid jumped through the floor into another
scene of workday devastation, and then down again. "We're
catching up to her," I said. "She has to keep making these
holes. We just have to jump through them."

And indeed, as we dropped down to the third
floor, we could see Minnie below us on the second. She
pounded one last time on the weakened floor, opening
it up, and flew through. Seconds later, we crashed down
behind her.

Thanks to the height of the concourse, it was a two-story
drop. The caryatid's feet smashed into the floor, sending bits
of tile flying.

"You can put me down here—" I began.

"LET'S GET HER BEFORE SHE NOTICES
WE'RE HERE!" the caryatid bellowed.

Fortunately, the Corkers opened fire, which was probably the only thing less subtle than the caryatid. They were
arranged in a semicircle on the other side of a metal ticket
barrier, next to a parked train car. Behind them, Beale sat
on an iron cage with the London Stone secured inside it.
He had changed into a puffy white uniform that looked
familiar, but what with the whole magical-cork-creatures-
firing-guns thing going on, I couldn't quite focus enough to
place it.

As the guns rang out, Minnie repositioned her wrecking ball in front of her, using it like a shield. Ricocheting bullets smashed the TV screens showing train times and knocked light fixtures off the ceiling. Dangling wires sparked frantically, setting a newspaper rack ablaze.

As I watched from my hiding place behind the giant stone woman's back, I couldn't help thinking that Beale's attempt to destroy Minnie looked awfully sincere. On the street, he might have been putting on a show for any civilians watching from a distance. But here, where the security cameras were broken and there were no witnesses that anybody would believe, who was he trying to fool?

What with being stomped on by the caryatid and shot up by the soldiers, the tiling on the floor had peeled back in several places, revealing the concrete floor beneath. Minnie shot a beam of fire at it with her free hand, carving out a slab of concrete. She swung that slab in front of the wrecking ball as a new shield, which freed her to do something else with the ball.

She rolled it at the soldiers.

If it hadn't been so terrifying, it would have been impressive. With a giant ball on a torn-up floor, Minnie looked about to bowl a perfect strike.

If the Corkers could feel fear, their stiff, mottled faces didn't show it. But for the first time, Beale looked terrified. I suddenly knew: he was not in control of this situation.

Yeah, Beale was a big, stupid, hot-tempered jerk. He deserved a good talking-to, and probably a good yelling-at.

But unless Parliament had implemented the death penalty for jerkiness, he didn't deserve a rolling-over.

And that meant taking out the girl who controlled the bowling ball.

"ATTACK!" I yelled in the caryatid's ear.

CHAPTER 57

We charged forwards. Minnie spun around, but it was too late. We crashed into her, sending her and her concrete wall crashing through the row of metal ticket barriers. The concrete ball wobbled off course, banging into the wall.

Lying underneath the caryatid, Minnie shot beams at the living statue, but they simply bounced off. Her powers must not have worked on Coade stone.

She stretched her arm out and summoned the wrecking ball. As it flew towards me, I rolled off the caryatid and onto the ground next to her.

The ball whizzed above my head. Minnie swung it around again and smashed it into the caryatid, sending *her* whizzing above my head.

As the caryatid crashed into the wall and dropped to

the floor, Minnie jumped up. With her wrecking ball high over her head, she hammered the caryatid again and again, pounding her deep into the floor.

"MMPRH MPRH RMPH PHRM," the caryatid proclaimed. I couldn't make out the individual words, but it was probably something about how perfectly ordinary it was for a giant statue to be embedded face down in the floor of a train station.

"Now!" yelled Beale.

The door of the nearby train slid open, and a large wax sphere rolled out. Minnie glanced at it contemptuously and smashed it with her wrecking ball. As she did, Beale flipped a hood over his head, and I finally recognized his puffy white uniform. It was what Aunt Mel wore when she was gathering honey from her hives.

Uh-oh. I knew what was in that wax ball, and I almost felt sorry for Minnie.

A thick cloud of angry bees shot out of the wax, but instead of swarming around Minnie, they surrounded the concrete ball and began buzzing madly into it.

Grandma's house had once gotten infested by masonry bees, but it had taken months. These bees must have been bred in some sort of magical bee-breeding facility, because they managed to dissolve Minnie's weapons in a matter of seconds.

"Surrender," Beale said. "You'll save us all a lot of trouble."

In response, Minnie pointed a finger at the bees. Beale

looked confused, but I knew immediately what she was up to.

"The bees!" I called. "They're full of masonry. And Minnie can control—"

Beams shot out, enveloping the bees, and they coalesced into a single buzzing ball, which shot towards Beale. He lifted his gun, but as he stepped forwards to fire, he stumbled over his loose shoelace, costing him a fraction of a second. That was all it took for Minnie to smash the bee-ball on top of him, trapping him inside it. She flung it off to the side, and he went flying, too, still surrounded by bees.

The Corkers had their guns—but Beale was too busy screaming to bellow out orders, so the Corkers just stood there, gaping.

Minnie gestured to the London Stone. It didn't budge. The iron cage that held it must have kept out whatever magical force she was using. With a shrug, she pointed at the ceiling above the cage. A heavy chunk of it toppled down, shattering the cage.

With a casual *Come here* gesture, she summoned the London Stone to her, and she levitated towards the other end of the platform.

I was about to follow when I heard a shriek from Brigadier Beale. He was still trapped in the ball of bees, swatting wildly as they stung him.

"I'll get you out of there," I told Beale.

"Don't—OW! Don't bother with meAAAAAEE! Save the—OW! London—AH!—St—OW—one."

He was probably right. Saving the entire city was more important than saving one particular person. But I still had no idea how I was going to save London—and as my eyes fell on the smoking remains of a newspaper stand, I thought I knew how to save Beale.

I grabbed a still-smoking magazine in each hand and carried them over, walking carefully so that the last bit of flame smoldering around their edges wouldn't blow out. When I was in arm's reach of the buzzing sphere, I waved the magazines, wafting smoke towards it. Ordinary bees hate smoke, and it seemed magical ones did, too. A narrow gap opened up.

"This way. Quickly!" I said.

Beale lurched forwards, stumbled through the gap, and collapsed on the ground. I dragged him as far away as I could.

He looked up at me through narrow gaps in his swollen eyelids. "I guess I was wrong about you, Hyacinth. Now go. Stop her."

"I'll have better odds if I know everything you know. Did your father really try to take control of London Bridge?"

He nodded, then winced, as if even that slight motion hurt. "I was just a child. I looked up to him so much—and then he betrayed his country. That taught me not to trust anyone. And it taught me that children are fools. Let's hope I was wrong, because you're all that's left."

"I know how hard it must have been," I said, and I meant it. "But I kind of need more practical information right now."

"In ancient times, they would display the severed heads of criminals and traitors on London Bridge. The history books said it was as a deterrent. But my father figured out that there was an additional purpose. The steady dripping of blood kept the bridge charged and powerful. My father was a police officer. He had access to a morgue. But if this girl is getting her hands on severed heads, I don't know where they came from."

I thought I knew the answer. "She didn't need them. That's why her first theft was from the Roman amphitheater. The sewer system there—so much blood flowed through it, it must be charged to this day. So she and her accomplice filled it with water and soaked the very first stones they took in it. That must have . . . I don't know . . . activated them, magically speaking. But how do I stop her?"

"Use the—" His eyes began to flutter shut. He fought to open them again. "Use the shield. That's how they stopped my father."

"What shield? The concrete one? The bees ate it."

"No. The . . ." His eyes shut, and this time they stayed closed. "The Roman one . . . ," he murmured, and slumped down into a faint.

There was nothing more I could do for him. "Get him a doctor," I ordered the Corkers.

Then I headed after Minnie.

CHAPTER 58

$\mathcal{A}$t the end of the platform, where the train would normally leave the station, the cage that surrounded the building blocked the way, but Minnie had tunneled a hole in the floor under it.

I squeezed through the hole and onto the railway bridge beyond. "Stop!" I yelled. For some reason, Minnie wasn't interested in advice from me, her friendly neighborhood archnemesis. Instead, she turned around and shot a fireball at the concrete pillars that supported the bridge.

The bridge shook and lurched downwards, creating a lovely and inviting ramp straight into the river. Gravity, as thoughtful as ever, knocked me down and sent me rolling straight into the water.

The current spun me around and around as it swept

me forwards under modern London Bridge. It straightened me out for a moment, giving me a prime view of the deadly waterfalls plunging through Minnie's Old London Bridge. The roar was deafening.

The supports of Minnie's bridge loomed up before me. I grabbed frantically at the nearest one, but my hands were too wet to hold on.

An explosive current whipped me through an arch. I felt like a bullet going through a gun barrel, except that gun barrels are smooth metal instead of rough stone, and bullets don't bleed.

And then I was through the arch, and for a moment, I had a view of the river before me—and below me, thanks to the change of water level.

Then the torrent of water shoved me down, all the way to the river's murky bottom. I would have been fine if I had taken a deep breath before going under, but instead, I had emptied out my lungs with all the important screaming I had to do. By the time I could point myself back towards the surface and start swimming, I could already feel myself running out of air. I clawed frantically at the water. My lungs strained as desperately as my arms. The water should have been getting lighter as I went up, but everything was going dim.

Finally, I broke the surface, gasping and sputtering, and sucked in enough air to make everything bright again.

I wasn't more than twenty feet from the bank of the river.

I took a deep breath and started swimming. I could barely paddle my arms. I could barely kick my legs. But paddle and kick I did, with all my might, and when my limbs stopped listening to me, I lifted up my head to see how far I had gotten.

I was still twenty feet away from the bank. The current had me trapped.

I had been shot at and handcuffed. I had been attacked by living rubble and by a bascule bridge. Through it all, I had never even considered defeat—until now. My muscles were giving up. Maybe I should, too.

"If I stop kicking," I said to the Thames, "I can sink quietly down. Everything is peaceful at the bottom of you. Why shouldn't I be, too?"

Splash, answered the Thames.

No, not the Thames. It was a life preserver landing in the water next to me. I grabbed it first and wondered where it came from second. The rope attached to it tightened, pulling me towards the shore. On the other end of the rope, I could see a figure reeling me in, but it wasn't until I got closer that I could see who it was:

Dasra.

And behind him was Hungerford, jaws clenched around the rope.

The river didn't let me go easily. For every two feet Dasra and Hungerford pulled me forwards, I slipped back one. And every once in a while, Hungerford would forget himself and roar encouragement, letting go of the rope and leaving

Dasra to fight the Thames on his own. But eventually, I was close enough to grab an iron handle protruding from the embankment. Dasra reached down and pulled me up.

I lay panting and shivering on the ground. Dasra handed me Excalibrolly. "You left this behind."

"Thank you," I said. "And not just for the umbrella. You saved my life."

Dasra shrugged. "I still owed you a third of a life. Now you owe me two thirds of one."

"No, but really," I said. "I was ready to give up. It's harder to keep fighting when you don't have a friend by your side. So thank you. Both of you."

Dasra was a human being and the grandson of a lady. Hungerford was a lion and made out of stone. But they had one thing in common: they were both English. If I hadn't noticed that before, the way they responded to a moment of intense emotion made it obvious.

"Well," Dasra said.

"Hrm," Hungerford said.

"That's, um," Dasra added.

"Indeed, it's quite, quite, quite . . . ," Hungerford agreed.

There was a long pause.

"Mustn't keep the others waiting," Dasra said.

"Oh, yes, there's a, a, a big battle going on," Hungerford said, with obvious relief. "Hop, hop on."

Dasra climbed onto Hungerford's back, and I climbed up behind him.

"The sun's going down and you're freezing," Dasra said. "Do you want my shirt?"

"No, I'd only soak it through," I said. "I'll just get close to you. You're nice and warm." As soon as I said it, I felt myself blushing, which at least had the benefit of warming me up. Now it was my turn to fumble awkwardly for the right words. "I mean, you're—I—um . . . How about that battle?"

$\mathcal{M}$innie's bridge loomed high above us, but there was no direct path onto it from river level. Hungerford ran instead through a paved courtyard, up a flight of stairs, and onto Lower Thames Street.

In front of us stood an old church with an iron gate leading into a courtyard that opened onto Minnie's bridge. Mom and Little Ben and Oaroboarus and a dozen Coade stone statues were arrayed on the ground in front of the gate, blocking access to the church. And above them, Coade stone birds and angels swooped, blocking access to the air. In front of them, Minnie stood, hurling stones of all sizes but unable to break through.

As I climbed down off Hungerford, a voice called to me from the bushes. "Pssst!" Mr. Champney peered out at me.

"I believe I can break this stalemate, but all this violence is rather frightening. Can you get me into the churchyard?"

I nodded at a Coade stone naval captain, who stood aside to let us pass. "This way," Mr. Champney said, leading us through an archway beneath the church's bell tower. On the inside of the archway, two metal bands held an ancient piece of wood against the stone wall. Next to the wood was a tiny door, barely up to my waist.

Mr. Champney placed a small device on top of the wood. A tightly coiled spring stuck out of the bottom of the device, and an antenna protruded from the top. He produced a key, unlocked the tiny door, and swung it open, revealing an extraordinarily narrow flight of stairs.

He knelt down and squeezed through the door. I followed, with Little Ben and Dasra close behind me.

"What was up with that piece of wood?" I asked.

"It's from the ancient Roman river wall," he said. "Wood is not my specialty, of course, but I'm guessing that, as it once held back the river, so it now helps this tower hold back the river's power."

"So you believe in magic now?"

"And what was that gizmo?" Little Ben asked.

"And where'd you get the key?" I added.

"In a moment," Mr. Champney said. "First, what do you notice about the staircase?"

"Obviously, it's tiny," I said.

"Much tinier than the tower," Dasra said.

I started to see where Mr. Champney was going with

this. "So that leaves a lot of room in the tower for something else. But what?"

"Allow me to show you." We had reached the top of the steps, which ended at another tiny door. Mr. Champney opened it up and squeezed himself out.

We followed him through it, onto a balcony halfway up the bell tower. We had a lovely view of the river, but it was the fight below that attracted my attention. The Coade stone statues had backed Minnie up against the side of an office building across the street. She still had a wall of rock around her, but the statues were pounding at it, and Minnie was drooping. The battle would be over soon.

Mr. Champney didn't seem particularly interested in the fight. He gazed thoughtfully at the big clock that stuck out of the middle of the tower, a few feet below our level. It was as big as a car, painted in black and dark brown, with the numbers on the clock face in gold. "The road to London Bridge used to run past this very tower," Mr. Champney said, "and this clock has been here for centuries. Think of what it must have seen."

Reaching into his pocket, he pulled out what looked like a small remote control. He took a deep breath, as if he was steeling himself for a big decision. That, together with the sad but determined look in his eyes, sent a sudden chill down my spine, and I remembered the gizmo he had put on the Roman plank. The antenna must have been there to receive the signal he was about to send, and the spring must have been to push the plank out of its holder.

But the plank held back the powers of the river. Knocking it out of place was something the Precious Man would do. And that couldn't be Mr. Champney. The Precious Man was Minnie's father, and Mr. Champney was too old for that. Besides, his daughter had died in a fire.

But had she? "They both survived . . . initially," he had said. If his daughter had come out of it alive, that would still have been true.

"That's why Minnie doesn't talk much," I said. "She's your daughter. *Her lungs were damaged by the smoke.*"

CHAPTER 60

*I*nstead of answering, Mr. Champney pushed the button on the remote control.

Down below us, I heard a *SPROING*. The side of the tower that faced the street swung open and water gushed out, sweeping towards the statues.

"Stop!" I cried, leaping for him, but he gestured, and Little Ben, Dasra, and I were thrown backwards, held against the wall of the tower.

Below us, Hungerford leapt forwards, crashing into the last bit of Minnie's stone shield, and it crumpled—

—as the water flowed out onto the street, burbling past the Coade stone statues. It was ankle height, and most of its force was spent, and for a moment, they didn't seem to notice.

Then they began shaking, like somebody who had

touched a downed power line. They collapsed and lay there motionless.

Mom and Oaroboarus now stood alone. With a wave of her hand, Minnie sent two nearby rocks crashing into their heads, knocking them out instantly.

"Ah, that's a relief," Mr. Champney said. "I knew the city kept a magical reservoir in this tower. I knew stones absorbed magic. I *thought* that a sufficiently big charge would be enough to overwhelm any statues who stood in our way, but I wasn't positive. That's why I had to let them exhaust themselves in battle first, to make sure their defenses were down." He leaned over the edge of the balcony and called down to Minnie. "Carly, sweetheart, are you okay?"

Carly? My fierce tattooed magical nemesis was named *Carly?* That was such a friendly name. I thought she would have been something like . . . I don't know . . . Circe. Or Boadicea. Not that a Hyacinth was really in a position to demand mighty-sounding names.

Mene Tekel/Minnie Tickle/Carly gave her dad a thumbs-up. "Why don't you get the sheep?" Mr. Champney called down to her. "I'll keep an eye on our guests."

As Minnie busied herself below, Mr. Champney breathed a sigh of relief, and his body sagged, as if releasing some strong tension. Clearly, he thought he had won. If I was going to find out what he was doing, this was my last chance.

I knew that if there was one thing historians loved, it was talking about their research. Mr. Champney had made an amazing discovery—how the original Mene Tekel got her powers—and then had to keep it a secret. He must have been aching to tell the story. I just had to give him a push.

"You've betrayed everything you stand for," I said. "You've destroyed a thousand years of history."

He bit his lip. His face wasn't as expressive as Chapel's, but in his sad, watery eyes, I thought I could see the need to explain building up. I pressed on. "You should be ashamed!"

"Don't speak to me of shame," he burst out. "Do you know who started the fire that killed my wife and nearly killed my daughter? I did. I was smoking in bed, and I fell asleep. I was alone most of my life, and when love found me in my old age, I destroyed it. *That* is shameful."

"So you're going to punish the world," I said.

"No!" he said. "I'm going to *save* the world." The words were pouring out of him now, as quickly as the water had poured out of the tower, as if they, too, had been stored in a reservoir for years. "Decades ago, when I was first rising to prominence in my field, Lady Roslyn sought my help. I told her everything I knew about the legends associated with London Bridge. That's what I thought they were, at the time—legends. After she left, the newspapers reported strange things, about an implausible plot by a man named Beale, and I began to wonder if the legends had some truth in them. But I couldn't abandon the foundations on which my entire life was based.

"When I sat in the hospital, watching my wife and daughter hover between life and death, I could feel those foundations crumbling. It was precisely the sort of thing that *does* make you want to believe in magic. The legends Lady Roslyn had asked me about revolved around a book with the secret of eternal life, hidden in a place that could only be reached by a magical journey across London Bridge. So I tracked her down and demanded the truth. My wife and daughter were near death, and she gave me nothing but evasions and half answers. If she knew secrets that could save lives, how dare she keep them to herself?"

I didn't have an answer to that. But Dasra did. "Some information is too dangerous to share."

Mr. Champney didn't look convinced. "Too dangerous for me, but not too dangerous for her? That seems awfully convenient."

Down below, Minnie rounded the corner, a herd of sheep milling in front of her. Their fleece looked oddly smudged, like it was a hastily scrawled drawing. *It's fog*, I realized. Every sheep was surrounded by a little cloud of fog, clinging to them as they trotted.

Mr. Champney continued, "If she wasn't going to tell me, I was determined to find out on my own. I threw myself into my research, but I didn't succeed in time. My wife died. Carly survived. Finally, a year ago, in a centuries-old manuscript long believed lost, I found the full testimony of the original Precious Man. Like me, he had weighed the world in the balance and found it wanting. From his text, I learned how to inscribe words of power on my body."

Without lowering the finger that he had pointed at us, he rolled up his sleeve, revealing a tattooed arm.

"They look different from Minnie—I mean, Carly's," I said.

"You're very observant," he said, looking pleased that I had gotten the right answer. The historians I knew were always happy to see people learn things, and apparently that included evil historians. "Yes, my tattoos are cruder and less effective. If you learn a language as a child, you can master it far more effectively than if you wait until you're an adult. That also applies to words you place on your body. That's why I had to bring Carly into it; my powers were insufficient for the task at hand."

"You put her in horrible danger," Dasra said.

Mr. Champney nodded. "I did. But not by giving her magical abilities. By bringing her into this cruel, dangerous world as a mortal human. That's why I have to find that book—it's her only chance for true safety. And once I've given it to her, I'll share the secret with all mankind. Everlasting life for everybody! Never again shall anyone know the sadness I have."

"I am so sorry for what you suffered," I said. "But what you don't know is, there's some sort of horrible consequence to immortality. For every life you save, you unleash a terrible force into the world."

"And how do you know that?"

"Because," Little Ben said, "we got a message from Ben Franklin, my ancestor, and possibly my brilliant but unorthodox creator who forged me out of lightning in the very heart of a storm! Wait, what was I saying? Oh. Yeah. He warned us about the consequences. And the message was only between him and his descendants, so you wouldn't know about it."

"That information belongs to all humanity," Mr. Champney said. "If he shared it only with his descendants, then he was of the same Elitist cult that produced Lady Roslyn—and I cannot trust anything he says."

Minnie floated up. Mr. Champney smiled gently at her. "Sheep all ready, darling?" She nodded, and he turned back to us. "Excuse me," he said politely, taking her hand. They floated back down to the ground.

As he went, Dasra called, "Mr. Champney, Lady Roslyn is my grandmother, and if she knows the secret to immortality, she's never told me or my mother. Do you think she loves us any less than you love your daughter? Why would she keep it from us—unless there really was some horrible price associated with it?"

For a moment, a look of concern flashed across Mr. Champney's face. Then he shrugged. "Because she's an Elitist. She wants to keep things for herself. That's what Elitists do."

Dasra turned to me. "You see? I *told* you an anarchist was behind all this."

CHAPTER 61

With Mr. Champney gone, the force field that was holding us in place lasted only a few seconds. We fell down, and I immediately jumped to my feet. I was, I realized, feeling a little better. At least being held up by hostile magic had given me the chance to recuperate a little from my swim.

"Come on," I called, and ran to the trapdoor. We squeezed ourselves back into the tower and crawled down the stairs. By the time we all emerged on the ground level, Mr. Champney and Minnie had hooked the sheep up to a sleigh, loaded the London Stone onto it, and herded the sheep onto the bridge.

While Dasra and Little Ben pursued them, I checked on Mom and Oaroboarus. They were unconscious and covered with bumps and bruises, but I was pretty sure they were going to be okay.

Behind me, I heard a *ZZZZZAP* and a "Yowch!" I turned around to see Little Ben and Dasra holding their noses in pain, as if they had just walked into a wall.

"Dere's a bagical barrier," Little Ben said through his swollen nose. He stood at the spot where the edge of the bridge touched the ground of the churchyard and reached his hand out gingerly. *ZZZZAP!* For a moment, a wall glowed into life, squares of fire appearing in the air stacked like bricks. "Cool!" Little Ben said. "Also, ow! But bostly cool!"

As Mr. Champney and Minnie drove the sheep along the bridge, the little clouds of fog around them soaked into their wool, and they began to glow like a dozen little furry suns. Meanwhile, the lights of the city's buildings dimmed, until nothing shone in the night but the stars above and the sheep below.

Soon, the halo around each sheep was big enough to touch the halo of the sheep next to it, and they merged into a single bleating sun. That sun flashed so bright that I thought it would sear my eyeballs, and then it lifted up from the sheep and disappeared into the London Stone. Now the London Stone was glowing, but it was a quiet, seething glow, like an ember that has been burning for hours but could still burn for hours more.

Although . . . it was fog that had started that ember burning. And we had stopped Minnie from collecting anywhere near as much fog as she had wanted. Did that mean the London Stone was running on a half-empty tank? Could I delay her long enough to make it run out?

The sheep reached the first of the bridge's alcoves, and as the sled passed, the alcove sparkled for a moment, and across the entire bridge, fragments of stone twinkled in response.

And across the city, all along the Thames, a few scattered buildings twinkled back. Little Ben gasped in appreciation. "The White Tower . . . Westminster Hall . . . the Church of St. Bartholomew—those are the buildings that were already there when the bridge was first built."

As the sheep trotted on, the city fell dark. On the bridge, the twinkling shifted, as if different fragments within it were answering the glow of the London Stone.

A few more buildings shone forth and faded—and then the city burst forth into twinkling light.

"And *those* are the buildings that were rebuilt after the Great Fire," Little Ben said.

"Minnie built the bridge with stones from every age," Dasra said. "I think each fragment is tuned in to buildings from the same era."

I thought about Grandma's old-fashioned radio, which tuned into different stations as you turned a knob. Maybe London Bridge was an enchanted version of that, powered by fog and blood instead of electricity. And that would make the sled the equivalent of the dial that showed the station. I could bring it back to me, if only I could find the knob that controlled it.

But how long did I have? I glanced up at the clock that stuck out of the bell tower, but it wasn't especially helpful. It was spinning madly, as if it, too, was tuned to the London Stone and was frantically trying to keep up with the passing of years.

"The clock!" I yelled. "The clock is the radio knob!"

Dasra and Little Ben looked at me, baffled. I couldn't blame them—it wasn't a sentence that would make much sense if you hadn't been listening to my thoughts—but there wasn't time to explain. "Trust me," I said. "We have to stop that clock from spinning. NOW."

"Great," Dasra said. "All we need to do is strike it with a lightning bolt or a javelin. I seem to have left both of those at home."

"Ooh!" Little Ben said. "You know who's made out of lightning? ME! (Possibly.) KAPOW!" He pointed his finger at the clock tower. Nothing happened. "Darn it!"

Over on the bridge, the sheep were almost at the far end, and the hundreds of modern buildings along the Thames were shining so brightly, it was like daytime.

The brightest building of all stood on the other side of the river, at exactly the spot where Minnie's bridge touched the opposite shore. It was thirteen stories tall, made of glass and pink marble, and it would have been an ordinary twentieth-century office building, if it weren't for the ten-story opening cut into its front, making the whole thing look like a giant open door. Under normal circumstances, the opening just revealed a glass atrium, set back from the river, but tonight was not normal. Instead of the atrium, there was a giant, spinning vortex.

Minnie's bridge led straight into the vortex's heart, and she and her dad were nearly there.

I had to stop her. I didn't have a lightning bolt—but maybe I did have a javelin after all.

I unsheathed Excalibrolly and took careful aim, trying to remember everything Aunt Uta had ever taught me about playing darts.

And then I threw it.

CHAPTER 62

$\mathscr{T}$he umbrella flew through the air, straight and true, and when it crashed into the clock face, the minute hand swept over it, wedging it in place. The clock ground loudly to a stop.

So did the sled. Minnie and Mr. Champney climbed out and pushed it, but it wouldn't budge.

But the hands of the clock still strained against Excalibrolly. I didn't know how long it would hold.

Little Ben held out a tentative hand towards the bridge. *BZZT!* The barrier was still there.

What had Brigadier Beale told me? *Use the shield. The Roman one.* But there weren't any Romans in sight. In the churchyard, there were shrubs and a bench, and in the street, a bunch of statues and the detritus of battle—bits of brick, and a mangled HANDICAP PARKING ONLY sign, and a ripped-off car door, and . . .

Wait a minute. That handicapped sign.

Like every other handicapped parking sign I'd ever seen, it showed a person sitting in a wheelchair.

And like every other handicapped parking sign I'd ever seen, it didn't really show that at all. It showed a stick figure with a round thing. Everybody interpreted the round thing as a wheel—but it could just as easily be a shield. And the stick figure could be somebody falling in combat.

I thought back to the unusual number of handicapped symbols I had seen at the garage that held the Roman wall. I remembered the circles painted on the bascule chamber, which had seemed to contain and channel the ghosts of the crushed stones.

This whole thing had started with the power of gladiator blood. Could a rune of a person wielding a shield be the thing to counter it?

I picked up the signpost from the rubble and held it like a jousting knight's lance, with the handicapped symbol where the point would go. I strode to the entrance of the bridge.

As the sign touched the invisible barrier, ripples appeared in the air around it, as if reality were a clear pool and the sign had disturbed the surface. The circle on the sign rippled, too, transforming from an abstract blue shape to a metal shield, dented in some long-forgotten battle. "Stay close," I told Dasra and Little Ben.

We passed through the ripples and onto the bridge, and

the air around us filled with faint images and not-very-faint noise. Flickering ghostly horses pulled flickering ghostly carts, with loud whinnies and rattling wheels, while their ghostly drivers yelled at the translucent owner of a translucent cow that was blocking the way.

"What are they saying?" I asked.

"I think it's the same language as your lullaby," Little Ben said.

"Can we go through them?" Dasra asked.

"Let's try," I said, and walked through the figures as if they were mist.

The ripples we made when we entered the bridge had kept going until they reached Mr. Champney, who spun around and saw us. He placed one hand on the London Stone and pointed the other at us. For a moment, his hand and the London Stone pulsed in bright synchronization—

—and then the stone and his hand faded out. The phantasms all around us disappeared.

"Not enough power," I said.

He must have come to the same conclusion, because he yanked his hand off the stone and it flickered back to life wanly. The phantasms reappeared.

"We can go faster if you help me hold this," I said. Dasra and Little Ben grabbed the back of the lance, and we ran.

As we did, faint buildings rose up around us, houses of black wood and white plaster. The ghost traffic became narrower and slower, crowded by the houses into the center of the bridge. Meanwhile, the costumes changed. The long gowns that both men and women wore became more color-ful. The hems of the men's gowns got shorter, showing off tightly stockinged legs. "Fourteenth century," Little Ben said.

The clothes became more diverse, changing faster and faster. The babble of voices around us was still overwhelming, but it was resolving itself into syllables that sounded more like the language I knew.

"Fraysh ohnyons!" cried an onion seller as we ran through her.

"Frish ahnyyens!" called the next one.

"Fresh onions!" shouted the next.

"Oooh! It's the Great Vowel Shift!" Little Ben said. "We're up to the sixteenth century."

I was less interested in the vowels than in Minnie and Mr. Champney, who were a few hundred feet away. Their sled still refused to move, and the sheep stood motionless, legs paused in the air, frozen in time.

And then the sheep began to move in slow motion.

"Excalibrolly must be slipping," I said.

There was a final grinding noise from behind us, and a snap, which sounded terribly like Excalibrolly breaking.

And the sheep trotted once more. They vanished into the vortex, pulling the sled and the London Stone and Minnie and Mr. Champney behind them.

The specters around us disappeared. The bridge fell silent.

"Awww," Little Ben said. "I wanted to hear the beginning of non-rhotic pronunciation."

I didn't know what that was, but unless it meant "the terrifying rumbling of a bridge on the verge of collapse," Little Ben didn't get his wish. Instead, the bridge shook furiously. Stone chunks toppled off the edges.

"London Bridge is falling down," Dasra said.

"Not just the bridge." I pointed to the buildings along the bank. They, too, were shaking.

"London Stone isn't in London anymore," Little Ben said. "It's in . . . wherever that vortex leads."

"Then we'd better get it back," I said.

No longer content with losing bits around the edges, London Bridge began to collapse, starting at the side where we had first entered.

We turned towards the vortex and, the bridge falling away at our heels, we ran.

 feel like I should come up with suitably grand language to describe the experience of passing through a building-sized portal powered by centuries of magical buildup, but it mostly felt like being a sock in a dryer. I was whirled around and around, tumbling head over heels, with the only light coming in through a small window. Only instead of looking out into the laundry room, the window looked out into— well, I wasn't sure where. It was a little hard to make it out, what with my field of vision constantly spinning.

Finally, the spinning slowed, the window swung open, and we toppled out into a narrow alleyway. The walls of the alley were simple blocks of stone, but the ground was paved with a crazy amalgam of materials—big granite slabs and little pebbles, Roman tile and modern asphalt, bits of broken glass and worn hexagons of wood.

"I think the portal has sent us to another world," Dasra said.

"Like a dryer does with socks!" I exclaimed. The other two looked at me. "Well, *I* thought it was a good metaphor."

Behind us, the portal whirled. Ahead of us, from the other end of the alley, I heard bleating. "That way," I said.

The alley opened onto a vast square, paved with the same dizzying array of materials. The buildings were bizarre, too. At first, I thought they were striped, with hundreds of lines running from roof to ground. Then I looked again and realized that each stripe was a vertical sliver from a different building, just wide enough to include the front door.

The doorways were hundreds of different ages and styles, but each one had something in common: the address above it. "It's the number thirteens we couldn't find on the streets of London," I said. "They all ended up here."

The sled with the London Stone stood abandoned in the middle of the square. The sheep, now glowing more brightly than ever, milled around the square, nibbling on the few stray bits of grass that grew between the more dirt-heavy paving options. But other than them and us, the square was empty.

"Where did those two go?" Little Ben asked.

"They must be in one of these doors," I said. "Let's start opening them." I strode up to the nearest one, a bright green door surrounded by a redbrick arch. But as I was about to turn the handle, I heard an eerie noise from the other side—high-pitched laughter, combined with an occasional *boing*. I didn't know what it was, and I didn't want to find out.

"Let's try the next one," I said. Before I opened it, I pressed my ear to the weathered wooden door. It was silent—for a moment. Then whatever was on the other side began screaming furiously.

I leapt back. "What *is* this place?"

"Based on how brightly the sheep are glowing, it must be brimming with magical energy," Little Ben said. "They're still soaking it up."

Dasra turned around, taking in the riot of building styles, and gasped. "It's Thwonrtthreethreen Skwaforthree," he said.

"That's not as illuminating an answer as I had hoped for."

"Look." He pointed to the upper levels of the buildings in front of us. When the slivers that made them had been cut out of their original buildings, they had brought fragments of street signs with them. "Read them in order."

It looked like a random assortment of numbers and letters to me. "T-H-1-R-T-3-3-N-S-Q-U-4-R-3."

"Right," Dasra said. "I heard my grandmother mention it once. It's a legendary containment facility for the most dangerous magical objects in London. Now that I see it written out, I see where the name comes from. TH1RT33N SQU4R3. It looks like Thirteen Square, but you say it like it's spelled."

"Thwonrtthreethreen Skwaforthree!" Little Ben said. "Cool!"

The thing on the other side of the wooden door was still wailing. "Whatever it's called, I don't think we should let anything out," I said.

Across the square, a black door with a single brass knob swung open, and Minnie and Mr. Champney staggered out, looking pale and frightened. Minnie clutched an old leather-bound book.

Mr. Champney swung around to slam the door shut, but he was moments too late. Something slipped out behind him. I didn't see it, but I heard it: a cacophony of rattling and banging, like a bull running into a rack loaded with pots and pans. I had never known a sound could have hostile intent, but this one definitely did. It shot past Mr. Champney and rolled through the square, straight towards us.

"Uh-oh," I said.

Right before it reached us, it passed the alley and hesitated. (Add "hesitating" to the list of things I hadn't known a sound could do.) Then it turned down the alley and zipped off through the vortex.

Whatever the sound was, it was now loose in London, but we had other worries. Mr. Champney and Minnie floated towards us. Their tattoos glowed brighter than ever before. Like the sheep, they must have been soaking up the energy of the place.

"I'm so sorry to do this to you, children," Mr. Champney said, looking at us kindly with his watery eyes. "I tried to keep you safe. I warned you to stay away, and when you insisted on meddling, I sent you off looking for buildings you could never find. But you can't seem to stay out of trouble. All things considered, you'll be safer here."

"We'll starve," Dasra said.

Mr. Champney gestured to a door across the square, and it swung open. "In the course of my research, I learned quite a bit about what's kept here. Mostly it's horrible magical forces that must never be unleashed, but that door simply holds Dodgson's Pitcher. Get it, speak the name of any food or beverage, and it will issue forth from within. Now, if you'll excuse us. We have humanity to save." He and Minnie floated towards the alley.

CHAPTER 64

I had only moments to stop them from going, and all I had to work with was doors and sheep. My grandma had taught me plenty about sheep—how to shear them, what they ate—but if there had been a lesson on using them in a desperate last-ditch effort to overcome a magical enemy, I must have been absent.

Unless . . .

"Are you sure Dodgson's Pitcher works?" I asked.

"My research hasn't been wrong yet," Mr. Champney answered.

"But you're dealing with myths and folklore. Things get mangled in the retelling. If it turns out the pitcher only produces spoiled food or something, we'll starve to death, and it will be your fault. Let me go get it and test it out. Then you can leave us with a clear conscience."

"All right," Mr. Champney said, but Minnie interrupted. "It's a trick," she croaked. "I can see it on her face."

She had seen right through me. Well, it wasn't surprising that somebody who had words all over her skin was good at reading body language.

Maybe I could make it work to my advantage. I made my most sincere darn-I've-been-discovered face. I let my shoulders slump as though my plan had been foiled. "Fine," I said. "But there was some truth to what I told you. You really should check out the food supply before you leave us."

Mr. Champney waggled his fingers, and a giant clay pitcher flew to him from the open door. It wasn't like any pitcher I had ever seen. The lip curled up and backwards to form the handle, twisting in a dizzying way that reminded me of the Coadeway. The whole thing was large enough that he had to hold it with both hands, and heavy enough to bring him floating back down to the ground.

"Strawberries," he said to the pitcher, and a fountain of strawberries poured out. He tasted one. "Delicious. All seems in order, so we really must—"

"MOLASSES MOLASSES SYRUP SYRUP MOLASSES!" I yelled. A huge plume of sticky stuff erupted from the pitcher, coating Mr. Champney and Minnie both.

"What are you—" he began.

"CLOVER CLOVER CLOVER CLOVER CLO-VER!" I yelled, and the pitcher erupted into a volcano of green leaves. They clung to the syrup-covered librarian and his daughter, transforming them into human pastures.

Mr. Champney sputtered angrily, but I wasn't paying attention to him. I watched the sheep. They lifted their heads in the air, noses twitching. Leaving behind the meager grass they had been nibbling, they trotted up to the sticky, clover-covered pair and began to graze.

"Get away from me," Mr. Champney said, but the sheep ignored him. He gestured at them. Nothing happened.

"Sheep absorb magic, remember?" I said. "They'll soak up any force fields you throw at them."

"Shoo!" croaked Minnie. She tried to float up, but the sheep had her clothes in their jaws, chewing away and holding her down.

In a moment, she'd slip free. So I had to act fast. "MONTMORILLONITE! MONTMORILLONITE! MONTMORILLONITE!" A powdery gray mass spewed out of Dodgson's Pitcher, coating Minnie and Mr. Champney in a new layer, making them look like statues.

"It's a kind of mineral," I explained. "My aunt Mel told me about it once. It's technically edible, so I could ask the pitcher for it. But more importantly . . ."

The glow from the sheep shot out of their wool and into the montmorillonite. Little Ben gave an excited squeal and finished my sentence. "More importantly, *stones absorb magic from wool.* . . . "

Dasra nodded, impressed. "Which we saw happen with the London Stone on the bridge."

"Know what else I saw, Mr. Champney?" I said. "I saw the little trick you did with the Coade stone statues. You overcharged them."

The glow from the sheep kept streaming into the layer of stone powder, which grew brighter and brighter. I could hardly bear to look at it now. "Those words of power on your arm—they soak up magic, too, don't they? That's why you're so much more powerful in here in TH1RT33N SQU4R3. But how much is too much?"

Their tattoos flared so brightly, they shone through the powdered stone and the clover and the syrup and their clothes. I had to look away.

It's a good thing, too, because when the tattoos exploded, sending powder and clover and molasses and clothing everywhere, I didn't get anything in my eyes.

CHAPTER 65

$\mathcal{T}$he force field that had held us in place evaporated.

Mr. Champney and Minnie lay unconscious on the ground, completely naked and no longer glowing. Their skin was bright red but otherwise unmarked, as if the tattoos had blown themselves off their bodies.

The sight of two naked evildoers was pretty eye-catching, but Little Ben was only interested in one thing. He knelt down and pried the leather-bound book out of Minnie's hand. He flipped it open and showed us the handwritten front page:

Being a Full and True Account of Certain Remarkable Experiments of Benjamin Franklin, with a Complete Explanation of London's Magical Rivers and the Source of Their Powers, by Moira Herkanopoulos.

"This is it," Little Ben said. "I know it! This is the book that will tell me who I am."

"Herkanopoulos is my mother's maiden name," I said. "This might be the book that explains what's going on with my family."

"Great," Dasra said. "Now put it back behind the door, and let's get out of here."

"Seriously?" Little Ben said. "This is one of the most important books in human history."

"And yet somebody chose to store it here. If we don't know why they locked it up, we don't dare bring it out into the world."

"We don't *know* why it's here," I told him, "but we can guess. Ben Franklin said there was some terrible price to immortality. I'm guessing it has something to do with that living sound that Minnie and Mr. Champney unleashed. There's plenty of doors here, so why would they store the book and the sound in the same place? I bet it's a safety measure. I bet the book tells us how to catch the sound."

"Then let's read it here," Dasra said.

"That will take hours," I said. "London was already falling down when we left. How much longer can it stand? We'd better stop gabbing and get the London Stone back."

Dasra looked like he wanted to argue, but he held his tongue. I was impressed—I didn't know he was capable of that.

I could feel the adrenaline that had kept me going all this time ebbing out of my body, but Dasra and I managed to drag Minnie and Mr. Champney onto the sled, while Little Ben lugged Dodgson's Pitcher back to the door that had held it.

We harnessed the sheep back up to the sled. "Yah, sheep!" Little Ben cried. "Giddyap!"

"That doesn't work with sheep," I said. "Here, I'll show you. You stand behind their shoulder and walk forwards like this . . ."

Together, we herded the sheep down the alley and up to the vortex. *Time to be a sock again,* I thought.

CHAPTER 66

$\mathcal{W}$hen we were through being tumble-dried, we all spilled out onto London Bridge. It was in exactly the same almost-collapsed state in which we had left it. Time must have passed differently inside TH1RT33N SQU4R3.

Dasra turned to me triumphantly. "I was right!" he said. "We could have stayed there and read the book for BLURB BLURB GLUB."

I might have wondered why he had ended the sentence that way, but since I was standing next to him when the bridge finished collapsing and we both plunged into the Thames, I was too busy blubbing and glubbing myself.

I tried to swim back towards the surface, but something pulled me down. In all that spinning inside the vortex, my foot had gotten tangled in the lines of the sled. I tried to pull myself free, but the line was tangled tight, and I had no strength left to fight.

Everything began to fade to black. Only little gray dots were left, swirling through my vision. They were, I realized, the last, crumbled remnants of Minnie's bridge. My ears were full of water, and above the muffled river noises they transmitted—above the occasional *clang* of a distant boat hull—I heard a sound with surprising clarity: weeping.

It's the artists who carved all those stones, I thought. They had left something of themselves in everything they made, and Minnie and Mr. Champney had used not only the blood of gladiators but the sweat and tears of artisans to power the bridge. And now all that blood, sweat, and tears—the life's work of countless Londoners—was being swept away by the tide.

My butt scraped the bottom of the Thames, and I felt something poke me. With what would probably be my last movement ever, I reached back and felt what it was.

It was the chisel the weeping ghosts had given me.

It was all that was left of their work, and I was all that was left to remember them.

And I was going to be gone soon.

NO.

I felt the anger welling up inside me. *NO,* I thought. *NO. All that creativity can't be for nothing.*

And with sudden strength, I pointed the chisel at the nearest swirl of dots. The anger surged up from my stomach and through my heart, mixing as it went with my awe at the beauty those poor dead sculptors had carved, and my respect for their hard work, and my gratitude for the heritage they had created. And all those twisty, mixed feelings poured down my arm and through my hand and right into the chisel, and a glowing beam shot out of it.

When I had wielded Excalibrolly and Bazalgette's Trowel, I had sensed the magic within them. This time, I knew, there was no magic in the chisel. It was just a hunk of metal. The magic was coming from somewhere inside me.

The river lit up. The swirling bits of stone turned to swirling bits of flame. No longer tossed by the current but driven by some internal purpose, they spiraled and coalesced, seeking each other out, meeting up and fusing, as if it was their destiny to be together. The bits of flame became chunks of statues and chunks of wall and chunks of sarcophagi, and the chunks spun together and were reunited.

My lungs must have long ago run out of air. But I felt only strength as the churning Thames began to fill with reassembled treasures.

I became aware that I was rising up towards the surface. I looked down and saw a pillar assembling beneath my feet, pushing me upwards as it did. The ropes that were tangled around my feet snapped.

I broke the surface at the same time as Dasra and Little Ben. They looked down at the newly reassembled archway that had lifted them up. They looked at the river, filled now with a thousand years of stones floating improbably, as if waiting to be collected and returned to their proper places.

And they looked at me. My hand was still extended as the magic from within me finished its work and the last glow faded from the chisel.

"Amaaaaaazing!" Little Ben said.

"How did you do that?" Dasra asked.

"I think . . . ," I said, and stopped. It wasn't doubt that made me hesitate. I knew the answer with utter certainty. But I knew that once I said it, nothing would be quite the same again. For better or for worse, that's what happens when you learn a new truth about yourself.

Finally, I said it. "I'm a tosheroon."

CHAPTER 67

$\mathcal{B}$y the time the pillar and the archway dropped us off on the banks of the Thames, the Saltpetre Men had arrived. They wrapped us up in shiny silver blankets. They carted away Minnie and Mr. Champney, who had washed up onto the shore, still unconscious, each floating in a separate sarcophagus.

"Brigadier Beale iss in the hosspital," Inspector Sands said, "but he iss well enough to confirm your innossensse. He hass already released Chapel, and you are free to go. I trusst you will give yoursself a well-desserved resst."

"Absolutely," I told him. I caught Little Ben's eye and winked. "In fact, I think I'm going to go home and curl up with a good book. What could be more relaxing than that?"

Mom came running up and grabbed me in a tight hug. Then she reached out one arm and pulled Little Ben into it.

Dasra stood off to the side, awkwardly. I caught Mom's eye and, with a slight motion of my head, pointed him out to her. She reached out and pulled him in, too.

I was glad. I mean, despite everything he had done for me, he was still Lady Roslyn's grandson. I wasn't going to hug him myself. But if my mom pulled him into a group hug that I happened to be a part of, I wasn't going to stop her.

When we were done hugging, I stood up straight, cleared my throat, and turned to my mom and my friends.

"Come on, everybody," I said. "It's time to find out who we are."

Author's Note

$\mathcal{M}$ost of the places that Hyacinth and her friends visit are real, and you can visit many of them, too, although if you are a magical stone creature, please try to do it discreetly.

Borough Market has existed for about a thousand years, and you can still buy all sorts of delicious food there. You can check the opening hours at boroughmarket.org.uk.

If he's not off on some ad-venture, Hungerford can be found standing on a plinth at the east end of Westmin-ster Bridge. His fellow Coade stones can be found through-out the city. The less-than-subtle caryatid holds up the roof at St. Pancras Parish Church.

The engineers in charge of Tower Bridge run occasional tours into the bascule cham-ber. See towerbridge.org.uk for tickets. If you plan on using the bascule chamber to crush thousands of years of London's heritage into magically charged rubble, please ask for permission in advance, as the engineers may frown on this.

Tower Bridge bascule chamber

In the graveyard of St. Pancras Old Church, you can see the tree with dozens of gravestones clustered around it, as well as John Soane's tomb, which is said to have inspired the design of London's famous red phone booths. (Note that Hyacinth and her friends were able to get close to Soane's tomb only because the fence that usually blocks it was mysteriously absent. Please respect any barriers that are there when you visit.)

The graveyard of St. Pancras Old Church

At the Church of St. Magnus the Martyr, the clock that looked out on Old London Bridge and the bit of wood from the old Roman wharf are not the only relics worth seeing. Out in the courtyard are stone fragments of Old London Bridge. Inside the church is a scale model of the bridge as it would have looked in the time of King Henry V. While you're there, you can pay your respects to Thomas Farriner, the baker in whose oven the Great Fire of London began. He's buried within the church. Church hours and more information can be found at stmagnusmartyr.org.uk.

The building in which the London Stone used to be half-heartedly displayed behind scratched glass is no longer standing. This is because it was destroyed in the battle between Hyacinth and Minnie Tickle, although the history books will probably claim it was torn down by developers. By the time you read this, the London Stone may once again be on display at 111 Cannon Street, in a brand-new building. I don't know whether the stone will be more visible in its new home, but I certainly hope it's better protected against magical theft.

London Bridge alcove

Alcoves from London Bridge stand in Victoria Park, Bow, London E3 5TB. The park is open from 7:00 AM to dusk, 365 days a year.

If you want to get inside the Mount Pleasant Mail Sorting Facility, you have two options. You can commit a serious magical crime, or you can visit the Postal Museum that's housed there. While you're there, you can even ride on Mail Rail. (The Mail Submarine is suspiciously absent.) Book tickets at postalmuseum.org.

ACKNOWLEDGMENTS

I'd like to thank everybody who helped me with this book.

For taking the time to answer my questions: Huda Abuzeid, Lucy Hornby, Otis Jennings, Dan McKee, Eric Peng, Lucinda Shih, and Janice Tsai;

My agent, Joan Paquette;

My editors, Diane Landolf at Random House and Gill Evans at Walker UK, and the entire team at both houses;

Teme Ring, Matthew Brozik, Zeba Khan, and Georgina Kamsika for reading early drafts and giving me their feedback;

All my children's teachers and caregivers, but especially Laura and Sara;

My whole family, with special love and gratitude for Lauren, Erin, Joseph, Mom, and Dad.